Attack

and

Defence

John Creasey

HOUSE OF
STRATUS

This edition published in 2012 by House of Stratus, an imprint of Stratus Books Ltd., Lisandra House, Fore Street, Looe, Cornwall, PL13 1AD, U.K.
www.houseofstratus.com

Typeset by House of Stratus.

A catalogue record for this book is available from the British Library and the Library of Congress.

ISBN 07551-3521 0
EAN 978-07551-3521 9

Chapter One

Robbery With Violence

The youth looked fresh and pleasant, with fair hair, blue eyes, a nice mouth and a firm, square chin.

'It may be worth ten thousand pounds,' he said, 'but I don't see why I should pay all that when I can get it for nothing. Don't try to stop me, Mannering, or you'll get hurt.'

He took an automatic out of his pocket, and covered the man who sat at the other side of the desk. Stretching out his left hand, he closed it over a single diamond which rested on a pad of cotton wool. There were others, and these he picked up too, slipping them into an inside pocket, before backing towards the door.

'And keep your hands in sight.' There was no edge to his pleasant voice, no change in his expression.

Mannering kept his hands on the desk and moved his right foot to the press-button in the floor.

This office was at the back of Quinns, a narrow shop in Mayfair, where Mannering dealt in precious stones, *objets d'art* and antiques of great value.

If the youth were nervous, he showed no sign of it.

'I'm serious,' he said, and opened the door a couple of inches.

Mannering watched him, ready to pull a drawer open and get his own gun, but not while he was covered.

'All you'll get for this is a stretch in jail,' he said mildly.

'That's what you think.' The youth opened the door another inch, then tightened his lips. Mannering didn't like the glint which sprang to his eyes, and flung himself sideways as the youth fired. The roar of the shot and the flash came simultaneously. Mannering felt the hammer-like blow at his temple before darkness engulfed him. He slumped forward on the desk, blood spattering the blotting paper in front of him.

The youth pulled the door wide open. A short, elderly man was coming swiftly along the narrow shop, and the youth fired again. As the man collapsed, the youth swung round, leaping up a flight of narrow, winding steps. Reaching the first floor, he rushed to the first window he came to. It showed a sheer drop to the courtyard outside. He pushed the gun back into his pocket, flung the window up and climbed out. Lowering himself, he hung for three seconds at full length, then dropped. He found himself in a narrow passage, which led to a narrow street beyond. He raced towards it, and the two-seater coupe which was parked some distance from the corner.

He drove off.

At the end of the street, a girl stepped off the kerb, and then hastily drew back to let him pass.

He smiled and waved to her, and went on.

Superintendent William Bristow of New Scotland Yard frequently said that he was the most over-worked man in London. He had some justification. He sat at his desk on that late September afternoon, reading through a pile of reports which had accumulated because he had been out on a case during the morning. A sudden gust from the open window caught several of the papers on top of the pile and whisked them to the floor.

Bristow glared at them.

As he did so the door opened and a further flurry of papers rose from the desk and floated about Bristow like a sand storm.

'Shut that door!' he roared.

'Sorry.' A tall, lean man with a shock of ginger hair, advanced cautiously. 'Bill, there's …'

'I don't care what there is,' growled Bristow. 'Can't I have half an hour's peace? Do you have to run to me with every trivial piece of news? I'd like to know what the hell they pay you for.'

'Take it easy,' said Chief Inspector Gordon, gathering up the strewn reports. 'A friend of yours has been shot. We may have another murder job on our hands by tonight.'

Bristow stared. 'Friend?'

'You don't always admit it, but friend is the word.'

'Who?'

'John Mannering,' said Gordon. 'He was showing some diamonds to a customer, who shot him in the head, had a go at one of his assistants, and escaped by a window. Division's at Quinns now.'

Bristow said slowly: 'So he's caught it at last.'

His expression changed, and Gordon's mildly sardonic manner faded. There was plenty of character in Bristow's face now, a hardness which hadn't been there before. He said tersely: 'How long ago?'

'About half an hour.'

'Where's Mannering?'

'On the way to the Westminster Hospital.'

'Get them on the line, and find out how he is. Telephone me at Quinns, with a report. Have a man sent to Mannering's flat, to keep reporters and anyone else away from Mrs. Mannering.' Bristow slipped into his coat. 'Is he really likely to die?'

'The report was pretty grim.'

'No, damn it!' said Bristow, explosively. 'Mannering can't go out that way.' He saw something in Gordon's expression that he didn't like, and rasped: 'I know you hate Mannering's guts, but if I had three men with half his ability, we'd be a lot more efficient here than we are. Mannering's pulled off jobs we'd given up as hopeless, we owe him plenty and it's time someone said so. *I'll* say so.'

'I know Mannering's good, but I'm not so sure he's honest,' Gordon said carefully.

'Well, I am sure,' said Bristow. 'Tell the Assistant Commissioner where I've gone.'

He strode out, hurrying through the hall and down the steps to his car. Watched by the policeman on duty, he swung right along the Embankment, into Parliament Square, and then cut across St. James's Park.

He gave himself little time for thinking, but as he hummed past everything else on the road, impressions made pictures on his mind, like a moving camera which had picked up oddments out of the past and strung them together without any attempt at coherence or continuity. Mannering featured in them all. Mannering, when Bristow had first heard of him, as a collector of precious stones, amiable, helpful. A different Mannering, bleak and resourceful, under great pressure at the Yard – denying what Bristow and a few others had come to believe was true, that he was a jewel-thief who masqueraded under the soubriquet of the Baron. Mannering, threatened with arrest, laughing into Bristow's face and defying him – Mannering, breaking into strong-rooms and laying his hands on fortunes in precious stones.

He'd never known what had turned Mannering into a thief; and never known for certain what had turned him from crime. His wife's influence? That had something to do with it, but wasn't the full explanation. Mannering had been badly hurt, had struck out savagely, turned to crime – and seen its folly. The hurt had been healed, but he hadn't withdrawn at once. More pictures passed through Bristow's mind; of Mannering as the Baron, working against criminals who always appeared to keep on the right side of the law. Of Mannering robbing these rich crooks, and distributing what he'd stolen to a host of needy people. Then, later still, of Mannering working *with* the police, using his keen mind and his gift for detection for the protection of society.

There had never been proof that he had ever been the Baron. There was ample proof that without him, many dangerous criminals would still be at large.

Three minutes later, Bristow's car swung into Hart Row.

It was a narrow turning, with only a few shops on either side. Several police cars were parked there, and a little crowd had gathered about the shop doorway. Two constables stood on duty.

Among the crowd was a youngish, fair-haired man wearing an old sports jacket and a pair of grey flannels; he looked cherubic, with a round, chubby face and mild blue eyes.

'Hallo, Chief. Anything for me?'

'No,' growled Bristow.

'Does Mrs. Mannering know?'

'Lay off her, will you?' asked Bristow.

Chittering of the *Daily Echo* said: 'All right. He'll pull through, won't he?'

A constable opened the door of the shop. It was crowded with detectives, and Bristow recognized burly Harding, one of the best Divisional Chief Inspectors in London. He turned to him.

'What's the latest?'

'Larraby, Mannering's shop manager, has given us a description—the gunman wasn't more than twenty, apparently. Larraby heard the warning buzzer, shouted for the police and then hurried to the office. The door opened and he heard a shot—and the young man shot him in the leg. The only things stolen, as far as anyone knows, were some diamonds that Mannering was showing to the killer.'

Bristow snapped: 'Killer?'

'I didn't see Mannering myself, as an ambulance was here within ten minutes, but I'm told he was in a very bad way.'

Jameson, the senior assistant, a small, middle-aged man, turned agitatedly to Bristow. 'I must go to the hospital, I really must. There's nothing I can do here.'

'There is, you know,' said Bristow. 'You can help a lot, as Larraby's out of action too. I'll make sure you know as soon as there's any news.' He looked into the office, where a man was taking photographs and another was smearing the desk with fingerprint powder. 'Had this gunman ever been here before?'

'I don't recognize anyone from Mr. Harding's description,' said Jameson, 'but I'm out a great deal. Mr. Bristow, what about Mrs. Mannering?'

'I'm going to see her.' Bristow turned into the office. Behind the desk, just above Mannering's chair, was a portrait of Mannering. This had been painted by his wife ten years or so before, when he had been in the early thirties, and he hadn't changed much in the intervening years.

The handsome face, the keen grey eyes, seemed to be smiling down at Bristow.

That fancy was broken by a sharp ring of the telephone bell.

It was Gordon – and Gordon should have news of Mannering.

Chapter Two

Bristow Breaks The News

'Hallo,' said Bristow sharply.

'Gordon here, sir. The news isn't very good.'

'Just how bad is it?'

'He's on the operating table now, and may be there for several hours.'

'So it's as bad as that,' said Bristow.

'I've laid on a man to stand by, for when he comes—if he comes — round,' Gordon told him.

'Right. Don't forget to draw up a rota.' Bristow rang off, aware of Harding's curious gaze. He would have to take himself in hand, he was showing his feelings too much.

'It's touch and go,' he reported. Then he saw Jameson hovering by the door. 'But there is a chance.' He saw the relief on Jameson's face. 'Tell me everything you can, will you?'

Harding related all he had learned from Larraby.

'Make it a priority job,' Bristow said gruffly. He had a mind picture of the distress on Jameson's face when he had heard the news. Larraby, he thought, would take things even harder, for he had particular reason for gratitude, having once served a prison sentence for jewel robbery. Larraby had made good; as more than a few had done under Mannering's influence.

Chittering was waiting for him. He looked shocked. 'John, of all people. I still can't believe it. It'll be the very devil for Lorna.' He lit a cigarette and flicked the match away. 'Bristow, if there's anything, anything I can do to help find that gunman, just say the word. And I mean anything. How soon can I have a description?'

'Harding will fix it. Tell him I think we ought to put the story as big as we can.'

'Thanks.' Chittering hurried off, but he was not thinking only about his headlines. He had often worked with Mannering, and few newspapermen knew him better.

He looked almost as badly shaken as Jameson had, Bristow reflected, as he drove off.

Ethel, the Mannerings' maid, was in the kitchen of their flat in Green Street, Chelsea. She was singing. Lorna, in the loft studio, could hear her slightly off-key soprano, although the hatch was closed.

In a paint-daubed smock, she stood, now in front of a partly-finished portrait, eyeing it critically. Her dark hair was untidy, and she blew at a whispy curl out of the corner of her mouth.

The singing reached a higher pitch.

Lorna put her brush down with a sigh. It was hot. The old winged armchair was tempting, but if she sat in it now she would probably laze for the next hour and be late for John. She was to meet him at Quinns at six o'clock, and had to dress. It was nearly half-past four.

Ethel's voice called to her: 'Shall I bring tea up, Ma'am?'

'No, I'm coming down.'

Lorna climbed down the awkward step-ladder from the studio, and met the girl coming out of the living-room. Ethel was tall, plump and pretty; a misguided teacher had told her she had a promising voice.

There was a moment of quiet, and then her voice shrilled out to new heights. Lorna closed the door firmly on an imperfect rendering of 'My love is like a red, red rose', and poured out a cup of tea.

Just before five o'clock she heard the front door bell ring, and a few seconds later Ethel's heavy tread across the hall.

She recognized a man's voice.

Fear stabbed into her mind. She would never get used to the fact that Bristow had become more a friend than an enemy.

'It's the Superintendent, Ma'am. Mr. Bristow,' said Ethel.

It wouldn't be a social call, that was certain. Bristow might want some information about precious stones, and prefer not to go to Quinns or to summon Mannering to the Yard. It was even possible that John had started some investigation which the Yard had discovered, and Bristow was hoping to persuade him to leave detection to the professionals.

Lorna smiled as Bristow approached. 'Hallo, Bill. I didn't expect you.'

'Nice to see you, Lorna.' He added uncomfortably: 'This is one of the jobs I don't like at all, I'm afraid.'

She was strikingly attractive, he thought; her skin, nearly olive-coloured was without blemish. Even her dark eyebrows, which sometimes gave her an expression both sombre and aloof, could not detract from her obvious beauty.

'What *is* it?' she demanded. 'Is John—?' she broke off.

'Lorna, I'm dreadfully sorry,' he said. 'John's been hurt in a robbery at Quinns. He was shot.'

Lorna backed away in sharp distress. Bristow shot out a steadying hand. In a moment or two she was in command of herself again. But she was glad of his support.

'How badly?'

'They're operating now, at the Westminster Hospital. I've a man there, and the moment there's news, you will be told. They're doing everything they can.'

She said: 'Of course.'

'We're after the gunman, and we'll get him soon,' Bristow said. 'We'll need help from you, I'm afraid. We must know what John was doing recently, and who he's been dealing with. The diamonds stolen were from the Fesina collection. Larraby has told us a little, he wasn't so badly hurt.'

'*Josh* hurt?' This was nightmare.

'Only a flesh wound. Unfortunately he can't throw any light on it, except that he knows John had several offers for the diamonds. Other things may have been stolen but we haven't traced any yet.'

'I've never wanted to get a man so much or so quickly.'

Lorna closed her eyes. 'Bill, tell me the whole truth. He's not—dead?'

'He has a good chance, that's all I know.'

She looked at him blankly, then as if she had suddenly awakened, she moved purposefully to the door.

'Can you take me to him? Or drop me where I can get a taxi?' She didn't wait for an answer, going ahead down the stairs. Every movement showed that same, deliberate haste, as if she wanted to rush headlong to the hospital but kept telling herself that she must not lose her self-control.

Chapter Three

Headlines

The almoner was both helpful and understanding.

'I can imagine just how you feel, Mrs. Mannering, and it isn't any use pretending there's nothing to worry about. It *is* a dangerous operation. But Sir Donald has performed many equally dangerous ones with complete success.'

Lorna managed to keep her voice steady.

'Can you send a message to Sir Donald before he goes, asking him to see me?'

For the first time, the almoner hesitated.

'He is very preoccupied. Perhaps it would be wiser to wait.'

'We're old friends,' Lorna said.

'In that case, I've no doubt he'll see you. I'll send a message that he'll get as soon as he comes out of the theatre. Will you excuse me for a few minutes?' The almoner smiled as she went out.

Lorna stared, unseeing, at the wall before her.

She had painted Donald Law's portrait, two years ago. She remembered his hands, long, pale, sensitive, capable of movements of great delicacy.

She closed her eyes, seeing those hands moving and a knife blade flashing; and blood on it.

A probationer brought her a cup of tea. Unable to sit still, Lorna moved restlessly about the room. When the almoner came back, she swung round, acutely disappointed because it wasn't Donald Law.

'Will he be long?'

'I shouldn't think so, but you really don't want him to hurry, do you? He'll take just as long as he has to, and not a minute more.' The words were meant to be reassuring, but somehow they made the hideous truth even more vivid. John's life was held in those pale hands. If they faltered, she would never see him alive again. When the door reopened, she hardly heard it.

A short, thin-faced man came towards her. He was *smiling*. Would he smile if the news were bad?

He shook hands.

'I'm very hopeful,' he said. 'Very.'

She didn't release his hand.

'He's—he's doing well?'

'So far, and I don't see why he shouldn't pull through altogether. We have the bullet. A fraction of an inch nearer the front of the head, and he would have been killed instantaneously.'

'Can I see him?'

'For a few moments,' agreed Law. 'Then I've instructions for you—to go home and rest. You'll be told if there's any change in his condition, and if there's no change during the night, that will be the best kind of news.'

Chittering, a police constable and a little crowd of reporters were outside the Green Street house when she got back just after eight o'clock. She shook her head mutely when the questions came, and let Chittering, more a family friend than a newspaperman, walk with her upstairs. Ethel opened the door before they reached it. She looked paler than Mannering.

'Oh, Mrs. Mannering, I'm ever so sorry, I'm—' she broke off. 'Oh, Ma'am, he'll be all right, won't he? He'll be all right?'

'The doctors think so,' said Lorna. 'Don't worry, Ethel.'

'Oh, Ma'am, your mother's telephoned three times, a newspaper chap told her about it. She says she'll call again at eight o'clock. She wishes she could come up, but your father's still ill, and she doesn't want to leave him. Mrs. Plender rang, and Mr. Jameson …'

Chittering ushered Lorna into the sitting-room, and said: 'Gin, I think.'

Ethel made her eat some dinner, and Chittering stayed to answer most of the telephone calls during the next hour. Her own doctor looked in just after ten o'clock, and insisted on giving her a sedative. She didn't want to sleep because she might have to rush off to the hospital; but she slept.

Ethel stood by the bedside with a tea tray. Lorna blinked at her, momentarily forgetful, and then sat up abruptly, panic-stricken. Ethel was beaming.

'They've just rang up, ma'am. He's had a good night!'

Lorna said: 'Oh, thank God.'

The newspapers lay in a neat bundle beside the tea pot. Opened the headlines blared at her.

JOHN MANNERING SHOT
THIEF ESCAPES WITH £25,000 GEMS
THIEF SHOOTS FAMOUS JEWEL MERCHANT £25,000
DIAMOND-HAUL

Wincing, she looked away from them, but a photograph of Bristow caught her eye, and almost against her will she read:

Superintendent Bristow of New Scotland Yard, one of the Big Five and the Yard's expert on precious stones, said last night that John Mannering had done more than any other individual not connected with the authorities to help in the detection of crime. Thanks to Mannering, several clever criminals now in jail might have escaped. In his generous tribute to a remarkable man, Superintendent Bristow said that Mr. Mannering's knowledge of precious stones was probably unrivalled anywhere in the world.

An extraordinary mixture of pain and pleasure wrung her heart.

Chittering took a cigarette from Bristow's yellow packet, and sat back in his chair in the Superintendent's office. Newspapermen were seldom allowed to penetrate so far into the Yard. His round, deceptively child-like face glowed innocently, as he leaned forward.

'Any luck, Bill?'

'We know the thief escaped through the window, otherwise we haven't a clue. This is off the record, mind you.'

'For the record, presumably, an arrest may be expected very shortly.'

'Call it that. But there wasn't a fingerprint we can find in *Records*, nothing to help us identify the man except Larraby's description. According to that he's about twenty-one, five feet nine or ten, good-looking, lean, fresh-complexioned, with light brown hair. It could apply to thousands.'

'Not good,' said Chittering.

'Someone must have seen him when he escaped,' said Bristow. 'We don't know whether he went on foot or by car. Most likely he'd have an accomplice somewhere nearby ready to drive him off. Although he was looking at the Fesina collection, Larraby had taken two different lots in for him to see. This means he might have come specially for the Fesinas; on the other hand, he might have grabbed them simply because the moment for a theft was ripe. I'm trying to find out if any dealer or collector is known to be particularly interested in the Fesinas, but nothing's shown up. Do you know anything about their history?'

'I should do,' said Chittering expansively. 'I've spent half the night looking it up. They were collected by the Duke of Fesina in the seventeenth century, and stayed in the family until a few years ago. The latest head of the family sold them, being nearly broke, and the sale was off the record—no-one knows who bought them. About half of the diamonds turned up three months ago, and were offered on the open market. Mannering bought them. They were sold by Mr. Mortimer Bryce, solicitor, of Lincoln's Inn, on behalf of an unnamed client.'

Bristow said: 'You haven't missed much.'

'Mannering told Larraby that he would like to get the other half, and then dispose of the whole collection, but was prepared to sell if he got the right buyer,' Chittering went on. 'I've a suspicion that he thought there was something odd about the business.'

'So Larraby says. I've talked to Mr. Bryce, the lawyer,' said Bristow. 'He's promised to try to get the seller's permission to pass on his name.'

'Can't you make him give it?'

'No.'

'What do you want me to do?' asked Chittering.

'There's one angle I'd like you to play—the fact that the thief must have been seen by people in Hart Row, and we want to hear from them.'

'I'll fix it, Bill. If it's humanly possible I intend to find the thief, and I don't much care who gets hurt in the process. What's the latest from the hospital?'

'No change. There's an even chance, now.'

'Even if he pulls through, it'll be a couple of months before he's fit again, so we've about two months to work in,' said Chittering.

Chittering's piece in the evening's *Echo* was exactly what Bristow wanted. It named the side streets behind Quinns, and asked for information from anyone who had seen a young man near those streets at the time of the crime. The story was still on the front page.

Lorna read it.

Ethel read it.

Several million Londoners read it. There was a stop press item in every edition; '*Mannering's condition unchanged* at …' giving the hour. Chittering had just decided that it was time he had something to eat, when his telephone bell rang.

'There's a young lady here, Mr. Chittering,' said a doorman. 'She says she thinks she can give some information about the thief who shot Mannering.'

'Handcuff her until I get downstairs,' Chittering urged, and jumped up.

Chapter Four

The Car

Chittering hurried into the waiting-room, where the girl sat alone. She had, he noted appreciatively, clear blue eyes and naturally fair hair. She was tall, and had beautifully shaped legs, and was dressed with taste.

'My name is Chittering,' he introduced himself. 'I'm looking after the Mannering case for the *Echo*.'

'I'm not at all sure I can help you,' the girl said at once.

'We'll find out, if you'll tell me all you can.' Chittering offered cigarettes.

'I don't want a lot of publicity.'

'If you don't want publicity, why come here and not the police? They'd keep you out of the public eye.'

'Would you rather I did?' asked the girl.

Chittering laughed.

'Not yet!' He sat back in an armchair. He liked the look of her, and not only because she was attractive. She had a kind of frankness which appealed to him.

'I came here because I thought someone on a newspaper could tell me whether I need go to the police. There seemed no point in upsetting my parents unnecessarily.'

'Just what did you see?'

'I was in Liddel Street yesterday afternoon, about the time of the raid. It's just behind Hart Row. I was in a hurry, and stepped off the pavement as a small sports car came along. There was a young man at the wheel—rather good-looking, really. The car didn't slow up. He grinned and waved, and went on. He was certainly in a hurry, and he seems to fit the description you published.'

'This could be the man,' murmured Chittering. 'Brown hair, fair complexion—you couldn't tell me his height, of course.'

'He looked average, and he was rather thin.'

'Who did you look at harder—the driver or the car?'

She laughed.

'I certainly watched the driver out of sight, he was that kind of young man.'

'Can you describe the car?'

'It was a green M.G. with a fabric hood, I don't suppose I should have paid much attention, but I always notice sevens.'

'Ah. Sevens.'

'I used to think it was my lucky number,' explained the girl. 'There was a seven on the registration plate. I don't know the letters, except that the first one was L, and there were two more. It had one of those square number plates—the letters on top and the numbers underneath. It was L something and then something 73.'

At home, Bristow was mellow and mild-mannered. With skill and sympathy he drew the story out of the girl. Her name was Anne Staffer, she lived with her parents in a house near Sloan Square, and helped to manage her father's dress shop. She couldn't recall any of the other numbers or letters on the car registration plate, but she did remember that there was a small patch in the canvas hood, on the nearside corner.

'Look, Ma'am,' said Ethel excitedly, when she brought in the tea next morning, 'it says that they've an important clue.' She began to read. '"An attractive blonde walked into the *Echo* office last evening and lodged important information about the Mannering robbery. At the request of the police, the *Echo* is withholding the name of this informant, who is in no way connected with the crime but has most unusual powers of observation. 'Do you think they've got the man?'

'If they had, they'd say so,' said Lorna.

'The hospital hasn't rung up this morning, and that's good news, isn't it?' Ethel went on.

'I hope so, but I'll ring them,' said Lorna, stretching out for the telephone.

John had passed a 'comfortable night' and might regain consciousness during the day.

Young Reginald Allen woke up about the same time as Lorna Mannering, in his bedroom in a small flat in Knightsbridge. He got up and went to the front door, pulling the newspapers out of the letter-box. On each of three front pages there was a story about Mannering and the attack; and in the *Echo*, news of the 'clue'. Allen tossed the paper away, and laughed.

'How they lie!' He laughed again, but a little uneasily.

There was nothing special about this furnished flat, but it had three rooms and a modicum of comfort. He wasn't rich – and he wanted to be. As he shaved, he studied his face in the mirror, and what he saw pleased him. He could be sure of attracting the attention of almost any pretty girl; what else was a good face for? He knew that people took to him on sight. He'd had a good education and had lived well. He was quite sure of his own personal courage, and now he knew he had plenty of nerve.

He cooked eggs and bacon, made some toast, and breakfasted at leisure. At ten o'clock precisely, he picked up the telephone and dialled a City number.

A man answered.

'Read the papers?' inquired Allen.

'Never mind what it says in the papers,' the other man said. 'Just lie low, and you won't have anything to worry about.'

'I hope not—but I keep remembering that a certain gentleman named James owes me a thousand pounds, in one pound notes,' said Allen.

'You'll get your money.'

'By noon today.'

'Soon.'

'Midday,' said Allen. 'Don't make any mistake about it. And I've been thinking—we ought to get rid of that car.'

'If you weren't seen—'

'I like to be careful, and I want to make sure that they can't trace it to me,' Allen said. 'You'd better shift it out of the garage, if you want me to stay in for the rest of the day. But after today, I'm going out.'

'You stay there,' said the other man urgently. 'I'll fix the car.'

James Walter Morris, a man of forty-two, with thin, black hair and dark brown eyes, drove past the garage where Allen kept his car, and saw two constables and several men in plain clothes gathered round it. He drove on without stopping, but there was a film of sweat on his forehead, which hadn't been there when he had reached the garage.

He drove to Allen's flat, and parked his car some way off; it was an Austin 16, which few people would notice. As he neared the house, a young man approached him. He was grinning.

'Paying a personal call?'

'You're going to. Courtney, the police will be here in a quarter of an hour. Allen's in danger.'

Courtney said thinly: 'You sure?'

'I'm quite sure. The police were round at his garage. Allen will talk, if they get him, too.'

Courtney looked up at the sky, and didn't speak for a while. Then his lips twisted in a faint smile. He said lightly: 'Reggie and me have been buddies for a long time, but you're right, he talks too much.'

Courtney went along the street. The house where Allen lived was a four-storeyed one, and all the flats were self-contained. He went up to Allen's flat on the third floor, and rang the bell – three short rings and two long ones.

Allen, fully dressed, greeted him with a smile.

'Hallo, Bill, come in! Did Morris send you?' Courtney nodded, and Allen went on: 'I had a funny idea that he would be late with the dough—I must have wronged him! Have a drink, or is it too early?'

'Not now,' said Courtney. 'Is everything all right?'

'Any reason why it shouldn't be?'

'You haven't a girl tucked in bed here, have you?'

Allen laughed.

'Unfortunately, no. Morris couldn't get better service than that, could he? Nose to the job and all personal pursuits forsworn, temporarily. And don't forget, I'm good—not many people would have got away with. Mannering's stuff as easily as I did.' He led the way into the living-room, and turned with a sunny smile. 'Now, the loot, the jimmy-o'-goblins—don't say you haven't got them.'

'Oh, I've got them,' said Courtney. He put his hand to his inside coat pocket, and drew out a gun.

The bark of the shot broke across his words.

Chapter Five

Brick Wall

Mannering moved his right hand, very slightly, and smiled. He looked desperately ill. There were dark patches beneath his eyes, which had lost their brightness. Lorna fought back the sting of tears.

'Hallo, my darling.'

'My luck held,' murmured Mannering.

'Of course it held. Darling you're not to talk, or I shan't be able to stay.'

'Stay,' whispered Mannering.

When she left, half-an-hour later, he seemed to have dropped off into a doze. She needed no more telling that the battle was far from over, but the darkest shadow of fear had gone.

She drove to Quinns, which had been shut up for two days.

James unlocked the door and let her in.

She said quickly: 'I've just seen him. He'll be all right now.'

'Thank God for that,' said Jameson, simply.

'May I say how delighted I am—really delighted,' said a young man with a large, domed forehead. He was Peters, the latest junior. 'It's been a great anxiety, Mrs. Mannering.'

'Thank you, Peters, I know. How are things here?'

'I've just been talking to Mr. Jameson,' said Peters. 'We feel that Mr. Mannering would wish us to open as quickly as we can. Three gentlemen from the United States are expected today, as well as one from Paris, and I believe that Signor Benito is due from Milan, today or tomorrow. I had agreed with Mr. Larraby that, subject to your approval, we would open.'

'We can manage quite well for a week or two,' said Jameson. 'Mr. Larraby won't be in for some time, but if we engage a messenger, there should be no difficulty.'

'Right,' said Lorna, 'we'll open—it's past time I learned more about the shop.'

'But your own work—' protested Peters.

'I can do with a rest from it.' Lorna walked along the narrow shop to the office. She noted with a shiver that the blood-stains had been removed from the Queen Anne desk, the chair and the floor. A pile of correspondence lay on a silver salver.

Lorna spent an hour with Peters dealing with it, and had only just finished when Chittering arrived.

He greeted her warmly.

'Thanks to a girl with a pair of very sharp eyes, the police made a raid this morning on a gentleman named Reginald Allen. He was dead when the police arrived.'

Lorna paled. 'You mean he was murdered?'

'Yes, and that makes it a bigger job than we thought at first. There's no doubt that Allen came here, his prints tally with some the police found. Two of the smaller diamonds were sewn in the lining of his pocket, too. Apparently he worked with someone else, handed over most of what he stole, but kept those two for himself.'

Lorna said slowly: 'So it wasn't on the spur of the moment.'

'No, there's some kind of organization behind it. I have a feeling that Bristow has a feeling that it will be a nasty job.'

A week later, Lorna went into Mannering's ward, and found him sitting up.

He kissed her. 'I'm beginning to feel almost human again,' he said with a ghost of a smile. He went on a little querulously: 'Donald Law has been full of dire warnings. Apparently I'm to be here for another two weeks, and then a nursing home for two more. After that, he insists I should convalesce in the country.'

'Larraby and Peters are coping very well under the new manager,' Lorna said gently.

'New manager?' repeated Mannering, blankly. 'I'd rather close down for a few weeks than take a chance on a new man ...'

'It's not a new man, it's me!' said Lorna laughing. 'I promise I won't lose you more than a thousand or so a week.'

'But—'

'And I have a secretary,' said Lorna. 'The girl who answered Chittering's plea for help. Her father is retiring, so it all happened very neatly. The two men look after the shop, and I see the people you'd usually see. Larraby will be back in three weeks' time, so don't worry, darling.'

A nurse looked in. 'Only two or three more minutes, Mrs. Mannering, please.' She went out again.

'Marching orders,' said Mannering wryly. 'But you've left a happier man.' There was a gleam in his eyes as he went on: 'Is there any news from Bristow yet? I would like to know about the man who killed Reginald Allen.'

'We all would,' Lorna said; and shivered, because she knew that John was already longing to be in the hunt for the murderer of the man who had so nearly killed him.

For the whole of that week, a Mr. James Arthur Morris had searched every newspaper article about the Mannering case for any indication that the police believed that they could get beyond Allen. He found none. References in all the newspapers became shorter and shorter. The *Echo* kept it going more vigorously than any of the others, but at the end of the week, even the *Echo* had only a brief mention in one of the inside pages.

Morris, who had a small jeweller's shop near Hatton Garden and was believed to be honest, watched his assistant put up the wooden shutters. He locked the door, and walked briskly towards a bar near Leicester Square. Here he met Courtney.

'We'll soon be on to some big stuff,' Morris assured him, 'if you can fix the girl at Quinns.'

'I can fix her,' declared Courtney confidently.

Morris nodded his satisfaction, talked for twenty minutes, then left Courtney at the bar, going by Underground to his home in Ealing.

His wife, a plump and fading woman in the early forties, arranged a whisky and soda on the table by his chair, and opened the door to him as she had done every night for twenty years.

'Hallo, dear, had a tiring day?'

It was a nightly question needing no answer, and Morris looked round him with new eyes. 'We'll buy a bigger place than this, before long, my dear, and live in style.'

'Just as you say, dear. Shall I pour your drink, or will you?'

'I'll do it,' said Morris. He poured himself out a generous tot, and held it up to the light. 'Yes, business is going to be *very* good, from now on. I've started a new line.' He chuckled.

'I'm so glad,' said Mrs. Morris. 'Dinner's nearly ready.'

Morris smiled as he sipped his drink. He had taken a big chance, and it had come off. He had never trusted Allen's trigger-happy attitude, but Courtney was made of different metal.

He poured himself another drink, then picked up the paper. He saw a small paragraph that he hadn't noticed before. John Mannering, injured in the Mayfair jewel robbery, was now out of danger.

'Why should I worry?' Morris asked himself. 'If Allen were alive, it might be tricky. As it is, there's no problem.'

Like a shadow in the back of his mind was the fear that Courtney might become one; but whisky drove that fear away.

Chapter Six

Full Recovery

Lorna and John Mannering sprawled happily on the beach, the sun, warm and benign, beating down on to the sea and the distant cliffs. An Indian summer had lingered into early November, and this was the Mannerings' last day in Devon. It had been a restful, lovely holiday; one to remember.

All that was missing at Quinns, when they arrived the following afternoon, was the red carpet. Jameson stood ahead of Peters, and Sylvester and Anne Staffer stood behind them.

The greatest moment came when Mannering saw Josh Larraby just ahead of Jameson. Mannering gripped his hand.

'It's wonderful to be back,' he said a little huskily. 'Thanks, all of you.'

He went along to the office, leaving Lorna to talk to Sylvester and the girl, taking Larraby with him.

'And things are really going well?'

'Very smoothly, sir.'

'The girl?'

Larraby smiled.

'Until a few weeks ago I should have said that the last thing we wanted at Quinns was a young lady assistant, but I must say the patrons seem to like her. I expected some of our regular patrons to feel a little perturbed, but they haven't shown any sign of it. With the increasing volume of business, we could use her permanently.'

'Then we will.'

'I wonder if you'll tell her at once?' said Larraby. 'I think she is rather anxious about her future. I've had that impression during the past few days. It seemed to become more noticeable as the time for your return drew nearer.'

'I'll see her in five minutes,' said Mannering.

He sank into the chair in which he had been shot, and remembered everything that had happened as vividly as if it were taking place at that moment. Young Allen with his pleasant manner and his apparently genuine inquiries, then the gun and the realization that the youngster meant business. Mannering could recall the way his heart seemed to stop when he saw the fingers tighten on the gun; the way he had flung himself sideways; but for that, the bullet would have gone straight through his forehead.

Now, part of the Fesina collection was gone.

The insurance had covered that, so there was no financial loss. Lorna was probably right, and he was a fool to want to make inquiries, yet the compulsion had been working in him almost from the time that he had come round in the hospital. He was impatient to see Bristow, as impatient to see Chittering.

There was a tap at the door.

Anne Staffer came in. He liked the way she moved; there was a frankness about her eyes which he liked, too.

'Come and sit down,' Mannering said. 'I've a feeling that you like it here.'

'I do—very much,' she said warmly.

'And you'd like to stay?'

She clasped her hands.

'I'd give anything to be able to. I love the shop and the work itself, and I can't imagine anything I'd enjoy more. But I know you don't normally employ women, and I shall quite understand, if ...'

'Five hundred pounds a year until the end of the year, and a rise then if you're worth it,' offered Mannering unsmiling.

Her eyes glowed. 'Oh, thank you!'

Mannering leaned back, studying her. There was a hint of anxiety in her eyes, something he couldn't place. 'Happier now?'

'Much!'

Mannering said mildly: 'If you've ever anything on your mind, tell me—or tell my wife, if you'd rather. The job needs all your concentration, and you can't concentrate if you're worried.' He stood up and offered his hand. 'I hope you'll be with us for a long time.'

When she had gone, he sat back, frowning. She was relieved by this decision, but it hadn't driven all her anxieties away. Was there domestic trouble? A boy friend? He shrugged the thoughts aside, and started to look through some papers on the desk. There was another tap at the door.

It was Larraby.

'Come in, Josh,' said Mannering. 'And tell me how good it is to see me back again!'

Larraby smiled sedately. 'I didn't come about that. In fact I'm not sure that I should have come at all. I am a little anxious, possibly without reason. May I ask—?' he paused.

'Anything, Josh.'

'Have you engaged the young lady permanently?' When Mannering didn't answer, Larraby went on: 'I like her very much indeed, she does an excellent job and doesn't mind what hours she works, but—these last few days, I've had a feeling she had something on her mind. Sylvester blamed it on to the possibility that you'd dismiss her, but I'm not so sure. You see, sir, she's been followed from the shop several times in the past week or ten days, and I have a feeling that she's frightened.'

Chapter Seven

Boy Follows Girl

'Frightened,' echoed Mannering.

'I assure you I'm not exaggerating,' Larraby said. 'I deeply regret worrying you with anything like this just now, but I'd be wrong to keep it back.'

'You certainly would,' agreed Mannering. 'And it's good timing, Josh, I'm not in an office desk mood. A little mental exercise before I really settle down to work will do me a world of good. How long has this been going on?'

Larraby paused to consider.

'It began on the Monday of last week, precisely nine days ago.'

'And the follower?'

'Oh, a young man.'

'Attractive looking chap?'

'If it were simply a case of a persistent suitor, why should it worry Miss Staffer?' asked Larraby. 'I would say the girl is alarmed. *Frightened.*'

'Have you followed the chap?'

'Only a little way along Bond Street. I felt that if he were to be investigated, it should be by someone who won't be recognized as being from the shop.'

'I think I know just the man,' said Mannering. 'Thank you, Josh.'

'I did take one precaution,' Larraby said diffidently. 'I told the police-sergeant on the Hart Row beat that I was nervous here at nights, and he has doubled the patrol.'

'Nice work,' approved Mannering. He waited a moment and then dialled a Central number.

A girl answered: '*Daily Echo.*'

'Mr. Chittering, News Room, please.'

Almost at once, Chittering came on the line, brusque and businesslike.

'Chittering here.'

'And Mannering here.'

'John! You mountebank, why didn't you tell me? I'd have been on Quinns doorstep and you would have had a headline. How are you?'

'Fine, thanks. Are you busy?'

'Certainly I am. Aren't I a newspaperman?'

'Could you find time to look in here—just by chance?'

After a lengthy silence; Chittering spoke with a curious kind of mildness.

'You're not up to mischief *already* are you?'

Mannering laughed. 'We close at half-past five, and have tea at four o'clock. That's in twenty minutes.'

Larraby brought in tea on a Georgian silver tray, at four o'clock precisely. Lorna was pouring out the second cups, when Chittering arrived.

She pushed up a chair, and proffered a walnut cake.

Twenty minutes later, she left them to it.

Chittering lit a second cigarette, and looked at Mannering expectantly.

'Now what, John?'

'Did you know that Anne had a boy-friend?' asked Mannering.

Chittering said: 'I did *not*.'

'Could you find out if she has, and who it is?'

'I'm not paid to spy on young love.'

'I'm interested in the youth who followed her last Monday, Tuesday and Friday, and again this week,' Mannering said. 'Josh isn't happy about it. He thinks the girl's frightened.'

Chittering stopped smiling.

'Well, well,' he said. 'Josh doesn't scare easily. I'll see what I can do. Expecting the chap again tonight?'

'I think he is,' said Mannering.

Chittering saw the young man at twenty-five minutes past five, when he approached Hart Row from the Oxford Street end of Bond Street. He wore a well-tailored suit of dark brown, and smoked a cigarette as he studied the window of a silversmith's shop, not far from Hart Row. Chittering contemplated the window of a lingerie establishment; there were mirrors in that window, and he could see Hart Row.

Anne Staffer came out.

Chittering couldn't see her face in detail, but noticed the agitated way she hurried across the street, as if she wanted to avoid the young man. As she drew nearer, Chittering could see her expression, and did not like what he saw. Was fear too strong a word?

Anne turned briskly towards Piccadilly, and the young man followed her.

Chittering kept pace with them on the other side of the road.

Several times the girl glanced at a taxi, but all were engaged. She reached Piccadilly and darted across the road, but was trapped on an island by the traffic. The young man was able to follow. Chittering made a dash in front of a taxi, and reached the middle of the road two yards away from them. He noticed the young man speaking to Anne. There was a smile on his face, but it was not the smile of an anxious lover; there was something of a sneer in it.

Anne took advantage of a break in the traffic to reach the pavement. The young man was now only a few yards behind her. He kept one hand in his pocket, and seemed quite unaware that he was being followed in turn.

They reached Green Park.

A taxi came along, its hire sign alight.

She waved, with a touch of desperation, and it slowed down. The young man made no attempt to follow, merely waving sardonically as the car sped away. Nevertheless, Chittering saw that he was glancing at passing taxis. Chittering moved under the collande in front of the Ritz, where he couldn't be seen – and luck favoured him, an empty taxi came up.

'Straight ahead, and pull up past the bus stops. I'm Press.'

The driver nodded.

The young man was smoothing down his thick, wavy brown hair as Chittering passed. Soon, another empty taxi appeared, and the young man hailed it.

As it passed them, Chittering said sharply: 'Follow that cab.'

'How far?'

'Destination.'

The driver nodded.

Chittering sat back and marvelled at the things that happened to John Mannering, and his extraordinary gift for smelling out crime.

Chittering tossed a half-finished cigarette out of the window. He knew exactly where the girl lived, for he had seen her home twice. When he saw the next turn which the young man's taxi took, he needed no more telling where he was going.

He got out of his own cab, told the driver to wait, and reached the corner the precise moment that the young man's taxi drew up outside Anne Staffer's.

Chapter Eight

Mannering Pays A Call

Mannering sighed, with the contentment of repletion, as Lorna poured out their after dinner coffee.

'Still brooding over my follies?' Mannering asked.

Lorna said: 'John, it's absurd, but I'm worried.'

Mannering said soberly: 'I know, my dear. But even if I were to promise not to probe into the Fesina diamond business, it wouldn't work out. It's been nagging at me for weeks. I've been hoping against hope that Bristow wouldn't settle the whole business before I had a chance to get restive.'

'Oh, that's to be worried over too,' said Lorna, 'but at the moment the worry is Anne Staffer.'

Mannering looked more surprised than he felt.

'I could see she was on edge when we arrived,' Lorna went on. 'There can't be anything wrong, can there?'

Mannering pressed her hand.

'I can assure you that the situation's under control.'

'Then you noticed it too?'

'Josh did, that's why Chitty came in. He followed Anne tonight. Josh told me that a young man has been trailing her.'

'I ought to have guessed,' said Lorna. 'You're not safe to let out of hospital.' She laughed with relief. 'It's saved me the trouble of telling you all about it, anyhow. More coffee?'

The telephone bell rang as she spoke. She looked at it wryly, and then picked up the coffee pot, while Mannering took the receiver.

'Hallo?'

'John?' It was Chittering.

'A brief report, but well worth making,' said Chittering. 'The young man's name is Courtney. He has rooms in Linden Road, off Edgware Road. He followed Anne until she took a taxi. He took another and arrived ahead of her. When she arrived she nearly fainted at the sight of him. They went in together. I found out from a neighbour that her parents are away. Courtney only stayed for a quarter of an hour, and when he came out he was looking very pleased with himself. He is now having dinner at the Czech Restaurant in Edgware Road. I'm at a cafe nearly opposite.'

'Thanks, Chitty, that sounds interesting. Have you a car with you?'

'No.'

'Mine will be near Linden Road in about forty minutes,' said Mannering. 'I won't be any longer. Don't drive off in it until I turn up, will you?'

'Going to have a look-see?'

'I'd better see you first,' Mannering said.

He put down the receiver, conscious of Lorna's gaze. He could guess what was passing through her mind, but couldn't imagine what he himself looked like. She was seeing the gleam in his eyes which had first fascinated her so long ago; the gleam which seemed to invite danger and betray his readiness to go and meet it. She knew he would never alter, that this was part of him – and if it were to fade, he wouldn't be the same man. It hurt because it was a mood she could never share.

'So you're going out,' she said.

'Coming?'

'You don't want me.'

'I could tell you all about it on the way,' said Mannering enticingly. 'Then you could have a chat with Chitty while you're waiting.' He drank the last of his coffee. 'Ready in ten minutes?'

He went into the bedroom, unlocked a drawer in the wardrobe, took out a small tool-kit, changed into a coat with a large pocket in the lining, and took a blue scarf out of the drawer. He put on an old hat and pulled it low over his eyes, then went into the bathroom and cut strips of Elastoplast, which he stuck on to the tips of his fingers and thumbs.

When he came out, Lorna was waiting for him in an old raincoat and headscarf.

They went to a set of lock-up garages in Victoria, where Mannering kept an old Austin, then drove to Linden Road. Number 79 was some distance from the main street, and Mannering driving past it, saw Chittering lurking at the corner which turned left. Mannering drew up.

'Going in?' Chittering asked hopefully.

'I'm going to try. Is there a back entrance?'

'No, only a garden wall, about seven feet high.'

'Hmm. Encouraging. Will you two amuse each other for a while? I may not be more than twenty minutes. If our Mr. Courtney shows up, give me a shout. Do you know if he lives alone?'

'I had a chat with a nice little thing who lives on the next floor,' said Chittering. 'Yes, he lives alone—second floor. What is more, he usually goes out to dinner and stays until eleven or twelve o'clock. I hope you know that what you're planning is strictly illegal.'

Mannering smiled, squeezed Lorna's hand, and walked off. It was dark and the nearest street lamp was thirty or forty yards away. There was a glass fanlight over the front door of Number 79, however, and the number of the house showed up clearly. Mannering went up four steps to the front door, which was closed and locked. Chittering and Lorna would give him warning if there was any danger of his being interrupted.

He took out a strip of mica.

It could be used for many purposes, one of them being that of forcing a Yale lock. To an expert, that was the simplest task, and he had become expert years ago. As he worked the mica between the side of the door and the doorframe, he could approve, dispassionately, the speed and dexterity with which he worked. Presently the lock clicked back.

Mannering pushed the door open, and stepped inside.

A dim light came from a landing, another from the end of a passage which ran from the front door. He went cautiously up the stairs. He reached the second floor, where there were four doors; all but the bathroom were locked.

There was no sound in the house.

Mannering slid a pick-lock from his pocket, and opened a blade. The cold metal slid through his fingers as he inserted it.

There was a sharp click as the lock went back.

He pushed the door open and stepped into the dark room. Taking out a pencil torch, he moved the bright streak across the floor. A cricket bag was propped up in one corner, the wall above it covered with photographs of girls in odd poses with bright artificial smiles.

Mannering took two opened letters off the mantelpiece, each addressed to William Courtney. One was typewritten. He opened it. It was from Holroyd and Green, Exporters and Importers, of Manchester, and regretted that there was no vacancy in any of their overseas branches for Mr. Courtney; it was dated a month earlier. The stiffness of the phrasing suggested that there never would be a vacancy. The second letter was a lot of slush from Tweeny.

Near the golf clubs was a tallboy, all the drawers of which were locked. Mannering used the pick-lock again, working in a silence only broken by the click of each lock as it opened. The first drawer was filled with papers, and two small, black bound books. One was filled with the names and addresses of girls; the other, of men.

Mannering slid this into his pocket, and searched on. Bank statements showed that Courtney was nearly two hundred pounds in the red; that made understandable a note from the bank manager, asking him to call at his earliest convenience. The letter was dated three weeks earlier. Mannering opened a file of applications for different jobs, both at home and overseas – all carbon copies. A small portable typewriter on the floor by the desk told that Courtney had typed them himself.

All the answers were curt and decided; there was no work for Mr. Courtney.

His reputation in business circles didn't seem good; one letter actually referred to 'past incidents which made it impossible to offer Mr. Courtney any kind of position'.

In the next drawer Mannering uncovered a revolver and a box of ammunition.

'Well, well,' he said softly.

He picked it up gingerly, and opened the chamber; it was fully loaded, a .32 Smith and Wesson. The bullet that had nearly killed him had been a .32.

Coincidence?

Courtney might have a licence for this gun, but that wasn't likely; the police were chary with licences. He put the gun into his pocket, and closed and re-locked the drawers. If he stayed much longer it would be asking for trouble.

He went back to the landing. He might as well look round the bedroom.

It proved to be a fair-sized room with a curtained alcove.

The curtains were drawn.

As he moved forward, they were flung apart. A man leapt at him, smashing a blow at his head.

Chapter Nine

Safe

The blow caught Mannering on the side of his neck, but glanced off. He heard footsteps, and the slamming of a door; then there was silence.

He picked himself up, alarmed and bruised, but otherwise unhurt.

He switched on the light, glanced round and saw the safe.

'So that's what he was after,' he muttered.

The safe was small, and partly covered by the flowered chintz drapes of the kidney-shaped dressing table.

Kneeling to examine it he saw that it was an old fashioned model, which, with the right tools, would cause little trouble to open. The difficulty was, that his tools were not the right ones.

He took out the small tool-kit he had brought. There was a special pick-lock which might do the trick. It needed great delicacy of touch and keen hearing.

Twice he felt the pick-lock grip, and twice it slipped; then it gripped for a third time. Heart in mouth, he twisted gently; it needed steady pressure, too much or too little would make the key slip again. He felt the barrel turning, there was a sharp click, and the lock was back.

The second lock took less than half the time, and he soon had the door open. Inside were papers, and a small heap of jewel cases.

He opened the top one, to find three diamond rings. They were worth, perhaps, a couple of hundred pounds or so. There were others. All of them had been recently set.

He examined the jewels with professional thoroughness before putting them back. Among the papers were two packets of letters, and a glance at the first told him that they were love-letters. He scanned one; it was a desperate kind of letter, obviously from a married man – frustration, un-happiness and anxiety all showed in it.

Mannering put both packets into his capacious inside pocket, and closed the safe. There were scratches on the outside of the lock – scratches he hadn't made. The first burglar had been after something in here.

Jewels – or the letters?

Mannering moved to the front door, eager to be gone. As he did so, the telephone-bell rang.

Quickly he retraced his steps, groped for the telephone, lifted it, and said in a muffled voice: 'Hallo.'

A girl said: 'Bill, I can't get it tonight. You must give me more time.' She gave him no chance to answer, but went on in a tense voice: 'I've tried every way, I just can't get it, you must give me more time!'

Mannering said harshly: 'You've had plenty of time.'

The girl said desperately: 'I think I can get it in a day or two, some of it, anyhow. Just give me until Saturday.'

'I want to talk to you,' said Mannering, in the muffled voice.

'Bill, it's no use. I haven't …'

'Meet me at the foot of the Lower Regent Street subway to Piccadilly Circus station, in half an hour,' said Mannering.

He rang off quickly, then closed and locked the door with the skeleton key, and hurried down the stairs. Chittering loomed up from a neighbouring doorway.

'Okay?' he breathed.

'Fine. Be Interesting to know what Courtney does when he finds he's been robbed,' said Mannering, sardonically.

Lorna, waiting at the corner, got into the car and took the wheel. Mannering slid in beside her.

'Mind if we go to Piccadilly Circus?'

'I don't mind where we go, as long as it's away from here. Do you want me to die of fright?'

'Well, you *would* come.'

'That wound in the head must have turned your brain!'

'I think you'll think the risk was worth it,' Mannering said soberly. 'William Courtney is a blackmailer, and one of the girls he's blackmailing is to meet me at Piccadilly Circus.'

Lorna didn't answer.

'He also deals in jewels,' said Mannering, 'and has a .32 Smith & Wesson. Do you think Anne Staffer has a skeleton in her cupboard, and is being blackmailed? I think it was her voice.'

'Oh, *no!*'

'*A* girl telephoned, begging for more time to pay,' said Mannering. 'Courtney saw Anne earlier tonight, and it would add up.'

Lorna drove in silence to Piccadilly Circus. She found a parking spot in a street leading off Shaftesbury Avenue, and soon they were walking briskly towards the station.

'She's to be at the Lower Regent Street subway,' said Mannering. 'We'll watch from a distance, and if Anne turns up, we'll meet as if by accident.'

They walked round the circular promenade to the ticket office, and stopped by a bookstall. Mannering judged that the half-hour was up.

Five more minutes passed.

'No-one's coming,' Lorna said, and there was relief in her voice. 'You must have been—'

She broke off, for she saw Anne.

She was approaching from the other side of the subway, walking quickly, staring towards the entrance.

When she reached it, she stood looking about her, frightened, defensive.

Lorna said: 'I would rather anything had happened than this.'

'It's something positive to work on,' said Mannering. 'No progress can be made with mere suspicion.'

'What has she done?'

'If you talk to her, you ought to find out before the night's over,' said Mannering quietly. 'You're really fond of her, aren't you?'

'Do you want me to tell her what we know?' Lorna asked.

'No. You must look surprised at seeing her, notice that she seems worried, and offer help. We take her home, and I'm pretty sure she'll confide in you. It wouldn't surprise me to find that Courtney is making demands he knows she can't meet, and will soon suggest that she can take something from Quinns, or else tell him all about the door locks.'

Lorna moved forward. 'Why, Anne!' she exclaimed.

Anne turned to Lorna; at close quarters, her pallor was alarming and her eyes were feverishly bright.

'Anne, what's wrong?' Lorna asked. 'You look as if you've seen a ghost.' She took Anne's arm. 'What on earth's the matter?'

'I—I'm all right,' said Anne, but her lips were quivering, and she couldn't keep it up. 'I—oh, I'm in such a mess!'

Chapter Ten

A Lesson In Ballistics

Mannering put his wife and the girl in a taxi, then drove back to Linden Road.

Chittering was still there.

'Oh, you remembered me, did you?' he asked gruffly. 'Next time you choose me for a job like this, make it midsummer. I'm chilled to the bone.'

Mannering said: 'I had a feeling you'd think that way. Chitty, would you lose any sleep if you knew Anne Staffer were really in a jam?'

Chittering frowned; in the poor light, his face looked bleak.

'Is she?'

'Yes. Courtney's blackmailing her. She's with Lorna now, with any luck we'll know the story in a couple of hours. In those two hours, Courtney will come back, find out that he's been burgled, and possibly get in touch with someone else.'

Chittering said: 'I'll wait.'

'We want to find where any accomplice lives.'

'I wasn't born yesterday,' said Chittering.

'There's just time to have a quick one, I'll take over for half an hour, if you like.'

'Forget it, John.'

'I'll leave you the Austin. It's parked just round the corner.'

'Thanks,' said Chittering. 'Where shall I leave it?'

'At any parking place near Victoria,' Mannering said, and gripped his arm. 'Good waiting!'

Mannering walked to Edgware Road, took a tube train to Sloane Square, fetched the Lagonda from the garage near Green Street, and drove to the C.I.D. building on the Embankment.

The officer on night-duty was Chief Inspector Pellew. He was fair, plump, ingenious, and a snare to unsuspecting crooks.

'Well, well, you haven't lost much time,' he said, pleasantly. 'Sit down, Mr. Mannering and tell me all your troubles!'

'Troubles?' echoed Mannering. 'What are they?'

'Now, now. You wouldn't come here at half-past ten at night simply to say hallo.'

'Want to find the gunman?'

'I don't mind telling you that we've been working pretty hard to do just that,' declared Pellew fervently.

'You know the bullet that was dug out of my head.'

'Do I!'

'Any pictures of it in Ballistics?'

'Yes, plenty,' replied Pellew. 'I don't see any harm in letting you see them, if that's what you want.'

He lumbered out, leaving Mannering alone in the office.

Pellew could have telephoned Ballistics for the photographs, Mannering thought with a grin. Going himself was more than likely to be a ruse for telephoning Bristow.

One cigarette was finished, and another started before Pellew was back, with half a dozen glossy prints. He pretended that he'd had a hard job finding them, and spread them out on his desk.

'If anyone uses that gun again we'll be able to match up,' Pellew said. 'What do you want to see these for, Mr. Mannering?'

'Can I have a souvenir of the bullet that nearly killed me?'

'Have 'em all,' said Pellew generously. 'And then make up your mind to tell us why you really want them.' He must know that Mannering wanted to check a bullet against them, of course. Bristow must have told him to be helpful.

'I certainly will,' said Mannering. 'No trace of the Festina diamonds coming on the market, I suppose?'

'Absolutely none.'

'Is any collector known to be interested in them?'

'I wouldn't know,' said Pellew. 'Bristow might, that's his cup of tea.'

'I'll have a chat with him in the morning,' said Mannering. 'Thank him for being so helpful, won't you?'

'What about thanking *me?*' demanded Pellew, and they both laughed.

Mannering garaged the car near the flat and walked along Green Street. He went upstairs quietly using his latch key. Rummaging in a store cupboard, he took out an old car rug and a block of wood, left behind when some joists had been repaired. He stood the block of wood against the door to the larder, and wrapped the gun round with strips of the car rug.

The scene set, he carefully fired the gun: there was a muffled report as the bullet smacked into the block of wood.

He unwrapped the pieces of rug, and opened the window, to let out the smell of burning wood and cotton. Then he took out a small steel vice, fixed the wood block in it, and sawed in the line of the bullet, on each side. He took a hammer and tapped the wood between the lines sharply, and a piece fell out.

The bullet fell with it.

He tidied up the kitchen, and went into his study. He could hear Lorna and the girl talking as he passed the sitting-room door. He sat at his desk and switched on the special light above it, took out a magnifying glass, held the bullet with a pair of tweezers, and examined it. The lines of the rifling showed up clearly.

He spread the pictures out on the desk, and compared them with the magnified picture of the bullet from Courtney's gun.

He could not be absolutely sure, but thought that Bristow would find that the bullet he had just fired, and the one taken from his head, would match up.

It looked as if Courtney had inherited Reginald Allen's gun; if so, he might have inherited other things. Mannering examined the notes he had made about the jewellery at Courtney's rooms, and compared them with recent lists of stolen jewels; none matched up.

He took out the love-letters.

He did not read closely, but looked for the signatures. The first one was Eustace. Eustace addressed a woman with every kind of endearment, but not her name. Nor was there an address at the top of the writing paper.

The other letters, even more passionately worded, were from a woman to a man. There wasn't much difference between one love-letter and another; the same passion unlocked the same words, the same mood of folly. There was no address on these either, merely the man's name, 'George', and the woman's, 'Win'.

He locked them in a drawer, and took out the address book. On the third page was an entry:

Eustace R. Staffer,
19, Conroy Street,
Sloane Square, S.W.

If this added up properly, Anne Staffer was being blackmailed because of a skeleton in her father's cupboard.

Mannering went into the living-room, where Anne Staffer was sitting. She had been crying, but was over it now.

'I hoped you were back, John,' Lorna said. 'Anne's told me what it's all about.'

'You've been so kind,' said Anne, warmly.

It appeared that her mother had a weak heart, and a shock might kill her. Her father had been blackmailed because of an *affaire* which had started, and finished, some years ago.

He had paid out so much money that his business had been ruined.

'When he just couldn't find any more money, Bill Courtney turned on me,' Anne said. 'He began about three weeks ago. I knew nothing about it until then, I only knew that father was worried—I thought it was because of the business. I'd saved a few hundred pounds, and Bill's had it all. He keeps wanting more. He waits for me nearly every night and tonight he said he must have a hundred pounds. And he's hinted—'

She broke off.

'That it would be easy to get something from the shop?' suggested Mannering.

'You guessed that?'

'It wasn't hard to guess,' said Mannering. 'He was using letters your father had written?'

'Yes. I just can't understand how father—' Anne broke off again. 'It's no use trying to understand, I only know that if mother finds out, it will kill her.'

'I'll deal with William Courtney,' said Mannering. 'You've nothing more to worry about, Anne, I promise you.'

He went on: 'Let Courtney think that you're still scared of him. Take his instructions, and report to me exactly what he wants you to do. He's lost the letters, but he won't tell you about that—so, officially, you don't know.'

'But how can you be sure?'

Mannering took the bundle of letters from his pocket, led her into the kitchen, opened the stove, and tossed the letters in.

As the last envelope flared and died, the telephone bell rang.

Chapter Eleven

Report

'Report,' said Chittering brightly. 'Courtney arrived ten minutes after you'd gone. He was upstairs, for fifteen minutes, and came down like greased lightning. Was that man frightened! He rushed to a telephone booth, then on to the nearest tube. I left the Austin, and followed. He got out at Ealing, met a man in a car on the Common, jumped in, and off they went. There wasn't a taxi in sight. So that's that.'

'Ealing Common,' echoed Mannering.

'The man who met him was driving a black Humber Hawk registration number 2HG513. I didn't really see the chap. Courtney just opened the door and jumped in.' There was a fractional pause; then: 'How is Anne?'

'If you happened to look in, before too long, you could offer to take her home.'

'Just give me half-an-hour!'

When Chittering arrived, Anne was actually smiling.

James Arthur Morris drove away from Ealing Common in his Humber Hawk. Courtney sat by his side, tight-lipped.

Soon they were in the open country.

Morris said thinly: 'I'm waiting for you to tell me what's happened.'

'I had a visitor tonight,' Courtney said.

'I'm not interested in your social life.'

'Nor was he—he wanted some letters. He took them, too, after opening my safe.'

Morris said sharply: 'Staffer's letters?'

'Yes.'

'Did he take anything else?'

'No.'

'Listen, Courtney,' said Morris, 'if you lie to me, you'll find yourself in real trouble. I look after you and you get well paid, but I want service, understand. What else was stolen?'

'I had another bundle of letters—'

'The jewels?'

'They weren't touched.'

'Whose were the other letters?'

'An old girl friend of mine.'

'Been blackmailing her too?'

'You should care.'

Morris said tersely: 'I do care. I told you to cut everything out, except Staffer, and when I tell you to do a thing—'

'I use my own judgment,' Courtney finished for him. 'I don't scrape to you or anyone else, and don't forget it. You pay me, but I do the work. If you're not satisfied, find someone else.'

Morris didn't speak.

'That's better,' said Courtney. He leaned forward, drew a flask from his hip pocket, and put it to his lips.

Morris said: 'That's all it wants.'

'I'll drink what I like, and when I like,' said Courtney deliberately. 'I promised to tell you if anything went wrong, and I'm telling you. It looks to me as if the thief came for those letters. It could have been the other man.'

'You said it was a woman.'

'They were written by a woman, to a boy friend.'

'What else was stolen?'

'Only an old address book,' Courtney said reluctantly. He didn't mention Allen's gun.

'Was my address in it?'

'Er … yes.'

'You bloody fool.' Morris pulled into the side of the road. 'Courtney, you're too clever for your own good. I don't like smarties who let themselves get robbed. If you leave address books and letters lying about—'

'They were locked in a safe.'

'Where did you buy it from? Woolworth's? They couldn't have got my address if you hadn't written it down. If there ever comes a time when you think you can start squeezing don't. Understand?'

Courtney looked at the jeweller in the faint light from the dashboard. His own pallor and the tension of his face were not visible; but tension sounded in his harsh breathing.

Morris went on softly: 'Don't make any mistake. I mean business. You do what I tell you, just that and no more. Is that clear?'

Courtney said sulkily: 'I couldn't help being robbed.'

'You could have helped putting my name in a book. We've got to get that book back. The thief did the job for Anne Staffer or for this other woman you've been blackmailing, so you've two places to look. Find out early tomorrow if Anne Staffer knows. You can easily tell. If she takes a strong line with you, it will mean that she knows she has nothing to worry about. For your sake, it had better be the other one, I've plenty of work for Anne to do. Properly handled, she can get a fortune for us from Quinns. Now, what's the name of the other woman?'

'Cartwright, Winifred Cartwright,' answered Courtney. 'The man she wrote the letters to is George Renway.'

'Where does he live?'

Courtney gave him the address, and: 'What are you going to do?'

'Find out if they have that book,' said Morris, 'and I don't want any help from you. Your job's with Anne Staffer. First thing in the morning, post those jewel cases to me at the shop—don't register them. Understand?'

'My hearing's good enough.'

'I wish your brain was,' said Morris.

It was too late for Courtney to catch a train, so Morris drove the younger man as far as Paddington, and let him walk from there.

Lorna woke next morning to find John sitting up, and the tea tray on the bedside table, with the morning papers.

She eyed him stonily. 'Two days ago I hadn't a worry in the world, but we had to come back to this.'

'It isn't *all* my fault,' Mannering pleaded.

'Most of it is,' said Lorna. 'You revel in it, don't you?'

'There's revelling, and justifiable revelling. Anne's feeling happier, Chittering is falling in love, and I think I have the gun that fired the fateful bullet.'

'*What?*'

'The problem is whether to tell Bristow that I stole it from Courtney, or not,' Mannering mused.

Lorna seemed too shocked to speak.

'He might suggest that we ought to have tipped off the police,' went on Mannering. 'On the other hand, by the time the wheels of the law had done their slow grinding, Courtney would probably have got rid of the gun, or used it again.'

'But John, this means—'

'It could mean that Courtney killed Allen, but Courtney could have got the gun from someone else,' Mannering pointed out. 'The real question is whether to make Bristow a present of the gun with an explanatory letter signed by Mr. Anonymous, or to say nothing, keep the gun, and at the proper time make sure that Courtney is caught with it in his possession.'

Lorna said faintly: 'Let me have my tea.'

Mannering handed her a cup.

'I give up,' she said. 'Don't you see what this means—they *are* still after something at Quinns, and they want to use Anne to get it.'

'The Fesinas might have whetted their appetites,' conceded Mannering.

'What are you going to do?'

'Pay a call on Courtney this evening, but not as John Mannering.'

Lorna said: 'I suppose nothing will stop you.'

Mannering pretended not to hear, finished his tea and got out of bed. 'See how fit I am—quite well enough to take on half-a-dozen toughs.'

'You'll have to tell Bristow something, John, he was so good when you were ill. Don't let him down.'

'I'm going to make a working agreement with him,' said Mannering, 'and set the seal of respectability on the Baron.'

Chapter Twelve

Working Agreement

Bristow's handclasp was cool and firm.

'John, it's good to see you. I'm sorry I was out of town yesterday.'

'So was I.' Mannering sat down in the office and accepted a cigarette.

'Care to tell me why you wanted those photographs last night?'

'I met a man who had a gun.'

'Was it *the* gun?' Bristow asked, sharply.

Mannering stretched out his legs. He looked indolent and handsome, and completely at peace with the world.

'If you knew an amateur detective who came across a little matter which he ought to report to the police, but which, if so reported, might lose a mackerel, to catch a sprat, what would you do?'

'So it's like that,' said Bristow.

'This detective doesn't know for sure that it's the same gun, he only guesses.'

'If he's the man I think he is, he doesn't make many mistakes over that kind of thing,' said Bristow drily. 'So you've really got your teeth into the job. Tell me as much as you want to now, and give me time to think the situation over. I shall make one condition.'

'What's that?'

'If I tell you I must have information, you're to pass it over without argument.'

'That's hard,' said Mannering.

Bristow said: 'John, you've played this lone wolf act for a long time and nothing I do will ever stop you. But remember I've been after the people who killed Allen for nearly ten weeks, and I don't know anything more about it than I did when I started. You've been at it twenty-four hours, and—' he broke off, and threw up his hands. 'Oh, it doesn't make sense!'

Mannering said quietly: 'Listen, Bill.'

He told of Anne Staffer and Courtney, omitting only his own unlawful visit. Bristow could read between the lines better than most. 'So it was really put on to my plate, Bill. I could hardly have lost it if I'd tried.'

'Sure about this Humber Hawk registration number?'

'Yes.'

'Is Chittering helping you?'

'He's still a crime reporter.'

'I don't know that I like it,' said Bristow gruffly, 'but I think you'd better follow your hunch for a bit. I can find cut who owns this car—but on what you've told me, I couldn't do anything to touch the owner.'

'How long would it take you to find him?'

'Ten minutes or so.'

'May I wait?'

'There's no real reason why I shouldn't give you the name, but from now on, I'll have to be after the man too.'

Mannering said quietly: 'Bill, I don't want or intend to have a head-on clash with you. If we could work together, you on the routine and daily grind, I taking the risks and going where policemen dare not tread, we would get the results more quickly. Can't we work that way? Remember that in the long run we want the same thing. Take this job. On the face of it, there's a gang and at least one killer, and we might uncover something very ugly indeed.'

After a long pause, Bristow said: 'I'll see what I can do.'

The Humber Hawk 'was registered in the name of James Arthur Morris, with an address in Hatton Garden. That was his office and shop. He lived at Ealing.

When Mannering went to Quinns that morning, Anne Staffer was polishing an old cabinet with much energy. She looked up eagerly, obviously wanting to speak to him. 'Soon,' he said, and went past her up the narrow twisting stairs to the store and workrooms.

Larraby was in the one with the best light, re-gilding a carved wooden frame. The picture was standing against the wall, a shaft of sunlight giving it all the glamour of Southern Italy. Mannering lifted it for a closer scrutiny. 'Nice, Josh.'

'I thought you would be pleased with it.'

'Where did you say you bought it?'

'Peggotty's, in Bethnal Green.'

'Peggotty? Didn't he do a stretch recently?'

'He came out three months ago. I always thought that he had the rough end of that particular stick, sir,' said Larraby.

'And this one too,' said Mannering, 'if he sold a five hundred pounds picture for—'

'Three-pounds-fifteen, sir.'

'Go and see him some time today,' said Mannering. 'Tell him what the picture is worth, and that he will get a fifty-fifty cut in whatever we get for it, after we've paid for the cleaning and overheads. He won't make much easier money than that, and while you're in the East End, find out if any rumours are circulating about a jewel merchant named James Arthur Morris, who has a shop in Hatton Garden and a house in Ealing. Take the small Leica, and get a picture of him if you can.' With a friendly nod Mannering went downstairs to the office, beckoning to Anne.

He closed the door behind her, waved to a chair, and stood looking down at her. He could understand what Chittering felt; this morning the girl had a freshness and charm which it would be hard to improve upon, and she looked carefree. The difference between her expression now, and yesterday, was startling.

'Well, how did it go?' he asked.

'Bill was waiting for me when I left home this morning,' Anne said, simply. 'He was friendlier than he's been for some time!'

Mannering chuckled.

'Then he started to talk about the letters, and climbed down from a hundred pounds to twenty-five. I said I'd get it by Saturday. That seemed to satisfy him, and he promised me he wouldn't worry me again until then. He looked almost—well, relieved.'

'He would.'

'Why?'

'Because he would feel sure that you knew nothing about the missing letters. Don't worry about the money. I'll look after that. Where is the rendezvous?'

'Oxford Circus,' she answered slowly. 'I suppose you *do* know what you're doing.'

'Yes, Anne, I do.' He looked up as someone tapped on the door.

It was Chittering, who beamed almost shyly at Anne as she went out, pushing a hand through his curly hair. He sat on a corner of the desk, looking down at the papers on the blotting pad, up at the portrait, then into Mannering's eyes.

'Did Anne tell you that Courtney button-holed her this morning?' There was a touch of anxiety in the question.

'Yes. You needn't worry in case she's mixed up with the ugly side of the business.'

'It's nice to have one's judgment confirmed,' said Chattering. 'My spies reported that you spent some time with Bristow this morning. Of course, you don't have to tell me what he said, whether you've declared war with the Yard again or are going to smoke the pipe of peace now and for ever afterwards, but I'll bet he didn't tell you what I can. A Mr. James Arthur—'

'James Arthur Morris, Hatton Garden and Ealing,' said Mannering.

Chittering said: 'My, my, you *have* got the Yard eating out of your hand!' He was very thoughtful. 'Well, I can even improve on that. Morris has a good reputation; he isn't liked but is believed to be honest. He has a lot of dealings with a Mr. Mortimer Bryce, solicitor, of Lincoln's Inn Fields.'

Mannering said softly: 'You're doing nicely, Chitty. It was Bryce who sold the Fesinas to me.'

'And Morris is hand in glove with him,' murmured Chittering. 'He may even know something about the man who stole them back from you. Going to see Bryce first, or Morris?'

Chapter Thirteen

Make-Up

Mannering opened the door of the flat and stepped into the full cry of Ethel in song. The kitchen door was open, and Lorna must be out, or Ethel wouldn't let herself go so completely. He saw her quivering back at the sink as it bent over a bag of potatoes.

He waited until a slight lull assured him she was about to launch into a fresh spate and that no time must be lost. 'Ethel, where is Mrs. Mannering?' Ethel swung round; potato peeler in hand. 'Oh, *sir*. You didn't half give me a start, sir. Mrs. Plender telephoned, and they had some tea together, and she said she'd be back by half past six, sir.'

Mannering went into the main bedroom, opened the wardrobe, and pressed one of the panels, revealing a hidden section. In here was a suit of old clothes. He took it out, and laid it on the bed. It was several sizes too large for him – but it wouldn't be when he was finished. He also took out an elaborate make-up box and put it on the dressing table. Then he went back to the study, and poured himself a drink. He sipped, then lifted the telephone.

Before he had dialled, Lorna had let herself into the hall. She thrust open the study door.

'Hallo, darling! Doing anything tonight? The Plenders wondered if we're free for dinner?'

'You could be,' murmured Mannering.

'So you're going out.' Lorna picked up the drink he poured for her. 'I was afraid of it. Tell me everything.'

'A tall order,' said Mannering lightly. 'But still, I'll do my best. Item one—Bill Bristow and I have a working arrangement. He will turn a blind eye on necessary occasions but can't speak for others at the Yard. Item two, we have found a friend of Courtney's—come and have a look at him.'

He took a post-card size print from his pocket and handed it to Lorna; this was one of several prints from the photographs which Larraby had taken with a small Leica camera fastened into the waistband of his trousers, when he had called at Morris's shop.

Lorna handed it back.

'Most unprepossessing. I don't like him at all.'

'But he has a good reputation,' said Mannering. 'He does a lot of business with Mortimer Bryce.'

Lorna caught her breath. 'The man who sold you the Fesinas.' Her cheeks were flushed and her eyes bright with fear.

Mannering picked up the receiver, and dialled a Hampstead number.

'Mr. Mortimer Bryce?' asked Mannering, His voice hoarse and uncultured.

Lorna watched him intently.

'Mr. Morris gave me a message,' Mannering went on. 'He said you must go to see him at Ealing at nine o'clock, it's urgent. He'll be back by nine, he's had to do a rush job out of London …'

Lorna put her empty glass, sharply and disapprovingly, on the table.

'Okay, fine,' said Mannering, and replaced the receiver. 'Mortimer Bryce will be at Ealing at nine o'clock,' he announced, his normal voice coming almost as a shock. 'Oh, that reminds me!'

He dialled the number he'd found in the address book, and as he listened to the ringing sound, Lorna had a strange feeling; that he was really happy, although she was so afraid.

Morris answered, and Mannering dropped into the assumed voice: 'Mr. Bryce gave me a message for you. He's coming at nine o'clock sharp and must see you. He won't be home earlier, he's had to hurry off on an urgent job. He says it's important, you've got to be in.'

'Who are you?' Morris demanded.

'I work for Mr. Bryce,' said Mannering.

He let the receiver fall back noisily.

'That's all very well.' said Lorna, 'but they may not believe the message. Morris will probably call Bryce and find out that it's phoney.'

'It's a chance I'll have to take. Chittering is watching the Ealing house and Larraby's keeping an eye on Bryce's. Larraby is to go off duty at nine o'clock. We'll learn what's happened.'

'So you're going to search Bryce's house,' Lorna said.

'With luck,' agreed Mannering.

'I'm frightened.'

'Not you,' scoffed Mannering.

But at heart, he knew she was; he could feel it in the passion of her kiss.

Just before eight-fifteen, the dinner cooked and washed up, Ethel left the house to visit her boy-friend.

By then, Mannering was in the bedroom, sitting in front of the dressing-table. The make-up box was in front of him, and he began to work on his face.

Twenty minutes later, Lorna would not have recognized him. Dark shadows lay under his eyes, lines narrow and melancholy ran from his nose to his chin. A thin rubber surface covered his teeth, giving the appearance of stain and decay.

Satisfied, Mannering took a roll of cloth from the bed, and began to wind it round his waist, like a cummerbund. Lorna took the end, and walked round him slowly. She had done this before, knew exactly the effect he wanted. 'Is that comfortable?' She fastened it with a couple of safety pins.

Mannering turned to the shabby, out-size suit. When he was dressed and stood and looked at himself in the long mirror, he was staring at a stranger.

'It'll do,' he said, judicially.

Lorna said abruptly: 'Are you going to take a gun?'

'Just in case of accident,' Mannering murmured.

'Courtney's?'

'Not this time.'

Lorna said: 'Darling, please, please be very careful.'

As she spoke, the telephone bell rang.

Mannering picked up the receiver.

'This is Larraby, Mr. Mannering. Bryce left, by car, just five minutes ago.'

Elated, Mannering slipped out of the flat, then walked briskly towards the point where Larraby had parked the Austin earlier in the day. It stood waiting. He unlocked it and climbed in, then felt in the door-pocket near him. There was a set of tools which no reputable motorist should know how to use.

He drove straight to Ealing.

Mortimer Bryce had much further to come, and Mannering judged that he would have twenty minutes grace. He left the car at the end of Willerby Road, where Morris lived, then walked along it. He saw Chittering emerging from the doorway of an empty house.

Mannering drew level, and murmured: 'All quiet?'

'Great Scott!' breathed Chittering.

'Has anything been happening?'

'Mrs. Morris left about half an hour ago, all dressed up. I heard her say that she wouldn't be later than eleven. Does Lorna know you're here?'

'I've a feeling that she thinks I'm at Bryce's place, I didn't tell her that his was second port of call,' said Mannering. 'Chitty, you're a better friend than I deserve, but ought you to stay here? If we run into trouble you'll have compounded a felony.'

'I'm just a newspaper man, I don't know anything about the fat stranger who walked past a little while ago, do I?'

Mannering chuckled, and walked on.

There was a lamp near Number 31, Morris's house, and Mannering walked through the double gateway, past the garage, reaching the back garden. A dim light spread from a ground floor window, there were none upstairs. Mannering went to the door, using his torch to examine the lock.

It shouldn't give much trouble – unless it was bolted.

He used his pick-lock. The lock clicked back after a few seconds, and he turned the handle and pushed – the door opened. He slipped inside quickly, and then approached another door, which stood ajar. By the light from the hall, he could see that it led into a kitchen.

Suddenly a brighter light shone out, and Morris appeared.

Chapter Fourteen

Meeting Of Friends

Mannering backed swiftly into the kitchen and pressed flat against the wall.

His heart thumped as Morris stood, hesitating for a moment, then returned to the front of the house.

Mannering moved from his hiding-place.

He heard a car coming along the road. It stopped, and a car door slammed.

Morris opened the front door, Mannering heard him say: 'I thought you were going to be late.'

There was a mumbled answer, and the two men, Bryce and Morris, disappeared into the front room.

Mannering stepped swiftly along the passage, he heard the murmur of voices, and caught the word 'drink'.

'Soda?' asked Morris.

'Thanks.'

A pause followed, as if each was waiting for the other to start. The sound of a glass being put on a table came clearly.

'Well?' said Morris.

'What's it all about?' asked Bryce.

There was another pause.

Mannering peered through the crack between the door and the door frame. He could see Bryce, a small, florid-faced man with stiff grey hair and a thrusting lower-lip, sitting bolt upright, staring up into Morris's face.

Morris's voice came sharply: 'What's gone wrong?'

The first signs of alarm began to show in Bryce's voice. He moved suddenly out of Mannering's vision.

'I don't get this. Why did you send for me?'

'*Send* for you?' the words rose to an incredulous squeak.

'Don't be a fool!' Bryce jumped to his feet. 'I had a message from you to say I was to be here at nine o'clock.'

Morris said: 'I—I don't understand. I had a message from *you*. You were coming here at nine o'clock.'

After a long silence, Bryce said softly: 'I don't like it, I don't like it at all. What time was this?'

'Six-thirty.'

'The same time as my message,' said Bryce. 'What's going on? Have you had any trouble?'

'Trouble?'

'That's right—trouble.'

Bryce was the boss, Mannering realized, Morris the hireling.

Morris said defensively: 'Courtney's flat was burgled last night, the thief stole an address book. My address was in it.'

Bryce barked: 'And mine?'

'How could it be? Courtney's only met you once, doesn't know where you live—doesn't even know your name.'

Bryce didn't answer.

'The trouble could be your end,' said Morris, cunningly.

'I don't let trouble happen,' Bryce said savagely. He leapt up.

'You see what this means? Someone wanted me out of my house, so they're probably inside now.' He thrust Morris aside and ran towards the door, wrenching it open.

Mannering said: 'Going places?'

Bryce stood stock still, his hands raised a little, his mouth agape. Morris, close behind him, made an odd little noise in his throat.

'There's no need to panic,' Mannering said easily. 'And you may as well be comfortable while you give me the information I require.

Bryce can sit in the leather chair, Morris in the blue one—and please keep your hands in view. I wouldn't like either of you to do anything exuberant, because my gun is very easy on the trigger.'

Both men moved mechanically to the chairs Mannering had indicated. Their mouths open, their breath coming short and huskily, they looked too stupefied to be dangerous. But it was a condition unlikely to last.

'Comfortable?' inquired Mannering.

Bryce swallowed hard. 'What do you want?'

'It depends what you've got. Rubies, maybe. Emeralds? I wouldn't even say no to diamonds.'

Mannering's expression was both sinister and grotesque. They would know that he was disguised, but that didn't matter; they couldn't guess who he was. The last time he had seen Bryce it had been in his office at Quinns, with the Fesinas scintillating on the desk between them.

'I don't understand you,' Bryce muttered.

'How about you, Mr. Morris?' inquired Mannering.

'I—I don't know anything about—' began Morris, and stopped abruptly.

'No? May I remind you, before you burst into any flights of imagination, that you are both very near to trouble. I don't think the Law Society would be happy about some of your activities, Mr. Bryce, and Hatton Garden doesn't like crooks any more than Lincoln's Inn.'

Morris said more sharply: 'What is it you want?'

'Supposing I tell you what I know about you?' suggested Mannering. 'Bryce, you've been selling precious stones which don't belong to you, and—'

Until that moment, Bryce's expression had been one of fear; now it changed, to a look of almost relief. Mannering noted this for future reference, and then went on before the pause became too noticeable: 'And you have been working through Morris, who puts the gems on the market. He cuts most of them down, and occasionally finds under-cover buyers for the really big stones. Morris, *you* handled the Fesinas.'

There was sweat on Morris's forehead and his long upper lip.

Mannering said: 'You were responsible for the job at Quinns, when you had Mannering shot. Remember Reggie Allen?'

Bryce shot a look of unbridled rage at his partner.

Mannering went on: 'Seven years in jail is about what you'll get at least. And what else do you think I discovered, Bryce. That it was you who sold Mannering the Fesinas, and Morris staked the boy who stole them back. How did you get the Fesinas, Bryce?'

Bryce said: 'I was acting perfectly legitimately on behalf of a client. Morris, is this true? You staked the thief, who—'

Morris said: 'You damned well know it's true!'

'Easy, gentlemen, easy,' said Mannering amiably. 'You're in it together, right up to the neck, not forgetting the attempted murder of Mannering and the murder of Allen. That makes it a life sentence for someone.'

Mannering looked from one to the other, unable to decide which of them was the more frightened.

'You needn't get excited about it, I'm not going to shop you, provided you behave yourselves. I simply want a cut in the profits. I'll take a thousand quid on the past jobs, and I want twenty-five per cent on the future ones. How does that sound?'

Bryce stared at Mannering intently. There was another change in his expression, one which sent warning to Mannering, one he must not ignore. There was a change in the atmosphere, too, an element he hadn't noticed before. He glanced up.

In the glass of a water-colour hanging over the mantelpiece, he saw the reflection of someone behind him.

Chapter Fifteen

Third Party

If Mannering moved round, Morris or Bryce would leap at him. If he stayed where he was, he was at the mercy of the man behind him.

He went on, showing no sign that he was aware of the newcomer: 'Just twenty-five per cent, you can't say I'm greedy.' He leaned towards Morris, gun thrust forward. 'It's cheap at the price. By the way, tell our friend behind me that if he starts any trouble, I'll shoot you.'

Morris gasped.

Bryce started to rise in his chair, and thought better of it. There was another faint sound behind Mannering. He could not tell whether the newcomer had a weapon.

'Just tell him,' Mannering said.

He stood upright, and began to move towards the left; if he could get to the side, he would be able to cover all three.

He was half-way to the wall when he heard movement behind him, saw a confused reflection a second before he was hit. It was a glancing blow but enough to push him off balance. At the same moment Bryce aimed a savage blow at his wrist.

The gun dropped.

Bryce smashed a blow at his face, Mannering fended it off and drove to the stomach. Bryce gave a belching groan, and backed away.

Morris was standing in front of his chair, with an automatic in his hand.

'That's enough,' he said. 'Don't move.'

The newcomer moved forward. The first thing Mannering saw was a foot – a woman's foot.

She kicked the gun across the floor, out of his reach.

He turned to look at her.

The woman was tall. A chiffon scarf hid her features, but she gave the impression of youth – and of authority, for quietly and quickly she took the gun from Morris's hand.

She held it downwards, and looked straight at Mannering: 'Who are a you?'

'Just a friend,' said Mannering.

'This isn't a game,' the woman said. 'Who are you?'

'Call me Uncle Joe,' said Mannering.

She glanced down at the gun, but didn't raise it. He thought that she hadn't much time for Morris or Bryce.

'You're really asking for trouble,' she said. 'But I can wait. You're heavily disguised, which means you aren't anxious to be recognized, but greasepaint can be cleaned off quickly enough.'

The shock was over, but the emergency was not. Mannering's curiosity was at fever-pitch. Who was the woman? And how had she evaded Chittering?

She turned to Morris. 'Just what happened?'

Morris told her, his voice nervous and staccato.

'He says that's how he got on to us, but I didn't know Allen had any friends who knew us.'

'There may be a lot of things you don't know,' the woman said.

Mannering murmured: 'But he knows who killed Allen.'

The woman spoke calmly, her voice muffled by the scarf.

'Do *you* know who killed him?'

'Ask Morris.'

'It wasn't Morris.'

'Nevertheless, he knows.'

Morris moved forward, swinging a left fist at Mannering's chin. Mannering took the blow on his shoulder, let Morris come close, and jabbed an uppercut. With all his weight behind it, the blow had tremendous power. Morris's head went upwards and back, his feet seemed to leave the floor before he fell.

Mannering straightened up, and rubbed his knuckles.

Bryce was muttering to himself, and did not appear to know what was going on. The house was quiet; it would have been almost reassuring but for the gun in the woman's hand. All Mannering could see was the vague shape of her nose and mouth. Shadowy darkness hid her eyes.

He smiled at her.

'Now let's stop fooling,' she said. 'Who are you, and what do you want?'

'I'm a man who likes to know when there's a fortune to be split up.'

'What makes you think these two know anything about a fortune?'

'My sixth sense.'

She tried another tack.

'How did you get in?'

'I opened the door.'

'You're a mobsman, of course. Did you break into Courtney's flat last night?'

Mannering said, with a look of assumed bewilderment: 'Courtney? Who is he?'

'If you don't know, you'll find out.' Her voice had a pleasant lilt, which touched a faint spark of recognition. He wanted to move the scarf aside so as to see her face, but her finger was on the trigger of the gun.

She said: 'How much do you know about precious stones?'

'That they're good currency in any language.'

'So that's all.' She shrugged. 'Well, it's time we had a better look at you. Bryce can you get up?'

Bryce stood up slowly, one hand against the chair for support.

'I don't think you're steady enough to hold a gun yet,' said the woman. She pointed to Mannering and nodded to an upright chair. 'Sit down.'

He obeyed.

There was another picture, a dark-background print, hanging low on the wall: it gave a better reflection than the first picture had done. He could see the reflection of the woman and some of the furniture, but not Bryce or Morris.

The woman came towards him.

He believed she intended to knock him out. He kept his gaze riveted on the picture, waiting for an agonizing second, then sprang up kicking the chair backwards, against her. She cried out.

Mannering swung round, and snatched the gun.

'Surprising what a difference a little bit of steel makes, isn't it?' he asked.

He lined Bryce against the wall, then turned to the woman.

'And now, lady, suppose we lift the veil.'

Chapter Sixteen

The Photograph

The woman stood without moving. He hadn't much time left; if Morris came round and Bryce grew bolder, the game could move the other way again.

She put her right hand to the scarf, and began, very slowly, to move it aside.

He wished she would hurry.

Her mouth came into sight, well-shaped, but determined.

Then suddenly she rushed across the room. He could shoot her, but couldn't stop her otherwise. She was at the front door by the time Mannering reached the passage.

He wouldn't shoot, and she seemed to sense it. She wrenched the front door open and darted out into the night. He was within a few feet of her, and made a final effort, hand outstretched. He clutched something, felt it give as she tore free and raced along the road.

A car turned into the road, its headlights sweeping the houses. If he were seen rushing after her, there would be trouble. He backed into the porch, acutely disappointed but admiring her courage; she had taken a desperate chance, and it had come off.

He went back into the house. What on earth had become of Chittering? But there wasn't time to worry about him now. Bryce and Morris gave him plenty to think about.

He saw a shadow from the room where he had left the two men. A bullet smacked a few inches beyond his head. Bryce fired again, and Mannering cried out, as if in agony.

Bryce came fully into sight, gun smoking. Mannering fired at it, and knocked it out of his hand, leaving the man helpless.

Then Mannering heard the sound of approaching footsteps and excited voices. He pushed Bryce back into the room, and slammed the door. The key was in the outside, and he locked it.

There was a thud at the front door.

'It was from here,' a man said clearly. 'I'm sure it was here!'

Mannering hurried through the kitchen to the back garden. There was a fence at the end of it, about five feet high. He climbed it, clambered through another garden, and found himself in a quiet and deserted street. Soon, he reached the end of Willerby Street where he had parked the Austin.

Chittering was nearby; he must be.

Chittering wouldn't have run out on him.

He started the engine, then slowed as a woman screamed. He saw that she was standing over the huddled body of a man: and feared that it was Chittering.

If Chittering were hurt, these people would give him attention quickly; he couldn't help the newspaperman if he were caught. On the other hand, if Bryce came out, he, himself, would certainly be recognized. He put his foot down and the car shot forward, but it was hard to make himself believe that it was the only thing to do.

There was one place of importance he hadn't yet visited, and there was time to do this, before Bryce took action. He sped along nearly deserted main roads towards the northwest, and Hampstead. He kept seeing a mind-picture of Chittering's face, so pleasant, so cherubic, so alive.

Who had attacked him?

The woman?

There wasn't much for Mannering to boast about, yet.

He left the car a hundred yards away from Bryce's property. He was a bachelor with two servants, the house, large and substantial.

Mannering walked quickly through the white gates, reached the big porch and shone his torch; that was taking a risk, but haste was all-important.

It would take him several minutes to force the lock of this door, but he would waste as many looking for a window he could force, or seeing if the back door were easier. His tools rattled as he drew the skeleton key out. There was little sound, and no light at any of the front windows.

The door opened.

He stepped into a dark hall. There was no light of any kind until he shone his torch; then he saw several big doors and a sweeping staircase; this was a large house, beautifully proportioned.

One of the doors was of the swing type. He went to it, and saw a light shining under a door on the right of the passage beyond. The servants, a man and wife, would be in there. He heard the faint sound of music from a radio.

He opened the door an inch, and peered through the narrow crack. He saw a man's feet comfortably crossed, and near them, a woman's.

He went back into the hall and moved a chair in front of the swing door. He saw a silver tray standing on an oak chest, and placed it on the chair seat; at the slightest touch it would clatter to the floor and give him plenty of warning.

He went through three other downstairs rooms, then mounted the stairs stealthily, his footsteps muffled by the thick pile of the carpet.

The second door he opened led to a study, a small, panelled room – the room of a man of wealth. A fire burned low in a wide hearth. It did not take him very long to find the safe in the wall behind a picture.

A combination wall safe was the worst type to open quickly; he doubted if he had time, nor had he the proper tools for such an intricate job. He turned away and approached the desk; that would be easier. He opened the middle drawer, with his pick-lock, careful not to scratch the surface.

He pulled out several papers, but found nothing of interest.

He thought he heard a sound.

He paused, his head raised. He went to the door and peered out cautiously; but there was no one there. There was no light downstairs and none on the landing. He went back and opened drawer after drawer in quick succession; none gave much difficulty.

Then he started to go through them.

In a bundle of papers were bills from James Arthur Morris, Jeweller. Mannering put those aside, and went on. He found some photographs in an envelope, and shook them out on the desk. Among the first he saw was one of Anne Staffer. He found one of Morris, another of Courtney, several of people he didn't know – men and women. There was only one other young woman, and she was a beauty; and vaguely familiar.

He turned it over, and read: Lady Iris Larmont.

He knew her slightly as a customer, and knew that her husband was a compulsive collector of precious stones.

This might be *the* clue he needed, for Lady Iris Larmont might well be the woman of Morris's house – that woman of authority.

Larmont, a widower for years, had lately married a girl who was twenty years younger than he. It had caused something of a stir in London Society, though she came from a good family, and there had been nothing really sensational. The Larmonts threw an occasional party, but did not enter into society with any great splash.

Mannering opened the last drawer.

In it was a file of letters to Mortimer Bryce, and each one was signed: 'Lester Larmont', They were instructions for the purchase and the sale of various jewels, and among them was an order for the disposal of the Fesinas.

The last letter was dated September 9th, just over a week before the attack on Quinns. It ran: I am very disappointed that you cannot persuade Mannering to sell the Fesinas back to you at the price he paid.

The matter is extremely important, as I have told you. If you cannot close this deal, I shall have to consider using another agent.

The tone was testy, the test a mystery; why sell jewels and then try to get them back? Why hadn't Bryce even tried to buy them?'

Mannering left the letters as He found them. There was no reason to let Bryce find out that the desk had been opened. He closed and re-locked the drawers, and stood up. He had the new angle he had been hoping for, the angle which had evaded Bristow, because Bryce hadn't talked about his working for Larmont.

Why not?

Possible answers flitted through Mannering's mind, and he rejected them. He went out, switched off the light, and closed the door. Darkness closed about him as he went down the stairs. He crossed the hall, took the metal tray off the chair and put it back on the chest, then replaced the chair, all by the light of the torch.

He opened the front door.

The glow of the street lamp met him; and silence. He closed the door gently, and hurried along the drive. Tension which had wrapped like a cloak from the moment he had realized that the woman would escape, was easing for the first time.

He opened the door of the Austin.

A woman inside said: 'You've been very quick.'

The street lamp gave sufficient light to show the gun in her hand.

Chapter Seventeen

Lady With A Gun

Mannering stood still for only a second; then he lowered his head and got into the car.

'Where would you like to go?' he asked.

She laughed; and her laugh was as attractive as her voice.

'You aren't a bit like your face,' she remarked. 'Just drive on to the Heath, a nice lonely spot.'

'Where lovers lie and the odd murder or two can be done by stealth,' said Mannering. 'I hope you haven't forgotten that I could have killed you.' He started off smoothly.

'I remember perfectly,' she said. 'I also remember that you hadn't the nerve to shoot.' When he didn't answer, she went on: 'What happened after I left Morris's house?'

'I made the silly mistake of thinking about two things at the same time, and forgot that Bryce was getting his breath back. He'd taken Morris's gun, and there was some shooting.'

Her voice sharpened. 'Is Bryce hurt?'

'I only meant to hit his gun, but I can't be sure his fingers didn't suffer. I don't think you'll find Bryce and Morris much good in the future, anyhow, their nerve began to crack tonight.'

He turned a corner, then came on to the Heath. Trees loomed up beneath the headlights, bushes grew close to the edge of the road, which was wide but twisting. 'Did you see a man in Willerby Street?'

'You mean, the man who was looking-out for you?'

'No one looks out for me, I work alone—but I knew he was there.'

She said sharply: 'How?'

'He's a crime reporter and has been interested in Morris for some time. I slid into the house without him noticing me, and when I left, he seemed to have run into trouble. I'm curious.'

'I hit him,' she said.

'You're quite an Amazon.'

'He was in the porch of Morris's house, and didn't hear me come. I hit him with the gun, and after that—'

She broke off.

'Yes?' asked Mannering, mildly — and he didn't slacken the car's speed. He had no illusions, however; the gun was covering him, and she was capable of using it.

'I dragged him into another porch.'

'He was still unconscious when I came away, so you must have hit him pretty hard.'

He felt her breath on the back of his neck; she was leaning towards him. He sensed that there was something he didn't understand, a trick up her sleeve. He moved his head forward, braced himself, and jammed on the brakes. The car shuddered to a standstill, the woman was shot forward.

He snapped on the courtesy light, and saw her lying nerveless, the gun in the left hand, a hypodermic syringe in the right. He leaned over and took the gun away, then took the syringe. He pushed her scarf aside.

She wasn't looking her best, but she was quite a beauty. Her name was Lady Larmont.

'You'll feel better in a few minutes,' Mannering said. 'Did you jab this hypo in to the newspaperman?' She didn't answer, but he could see that was the truth, and that she had had every intention of doing the same to him.

Mannering marshalled up all the facts he knew about her. She was the young wife of a middle-aged collector of precious stones who had sold his part of the Fesina collection secretly and then tried to buy it back. Bryce had been instructed to carry this out. but hadn't done so, using Reginald Allen's method instead. So far, that was logical. Bryce preferred to steal and to sell back to Larmont …

No, it wouldn't work; Larmont wouldn't pay for stolen jewels, and he must have known these were stolen, the story had hit every headline in the country.

Was it so certain Larmont wouldn't buy 'hot' stones? Many collectors did so if the mania for jewels took possession of them. They wouldn't care how they obtained what they wanted. He mustn't forget that, according to the letter, Larmont had wanted to buy them back.

His wife not only knew Bryce and Morris, but gave them instructions – each had seemed prepared to obey her.

'What are you going to do?' she asked presently.

He wondered what she would say if she realized that he knew who she was.

'I think you owe that newspaperman a break, don't you? We'll go and see him, and maybe he'll find a story in you.'

She was appalled. 'No!'

'Don't you like the idea of publicity?' He laughed harshly. "You'd make a good front-page picture, and the police would be interested, too.'

'You daren't do it.'

'What makes you think not?' asked Mannering. 'The police know all about the little fracas we had by now, they were arriving when I left. I don't know how Bryce and Morris will talk themselves out of it, but I am quite sure that if they're charged, they'll try to save their skins by blaming you.'

She said in a low-pitched voice: 'Bryce and Morris don't know who I am.'

Astonished, he said quickly: 'That's a tall one.'

'It's quite true. I have a hold on both Bryce and Morris,' she said. 'It pays them to do what I tell them. It will pay you, too.'

'But you've nothing on me.'

'It would still pay you to work with me.'

'I think in big money.'

75

'I work in big money.'

Mannering laughed. 'You certainly talk big, my pet. I'm interested, up to a point. How did you know about Courtney's flat being burgled?'

'I had Courtney watched, because I wasn't sure Morris was wise to use him.'

'Who did the watching?'

'No one who matters or who knows why I was interested.'

Mannering shrugged.

'All right, let's leave it at that. "Who are you, where do you live, and what's your racket?'

'If you think I'm going to give myself away as easily as that—'

Mannering said gently: 'My dear Lady Larmont—'

She started violently at the sound of her name; and for the first time, he saw fear in her grey eyes. Mannering patted her hand.

'All I want to know is your angle.'

She didn't answer.

'You don't have to tell me,' said Mannering. 'On the other hand, think of tomorrow's headlines. Lady Iris Larmont—'

'Stop it!'

'I might find it worth while on a fifty-fifty cut,' said Mannering, 'Now that Bryce or Morris are no good to you, you've only one chance of staying out of jail, and that is to confide in me.'

She still didn't answer.

'Please yourself,' said Mannering. He hustled her into the front seat, then took the wheel.

The girl sat absolutely motionless, by his side.

Mannering headed for the West End. It was nearly midnight and there was little traffic.

At last, she spoke.

'Where are you going?'

'Fleet Street. Didn't I tell you?'

'Take me to my home,' she said. 'I will tell you what it's all about.'

Chapter Eighteen

Whole Truth

The house was a big one in Grayling Square. The whole facade was in darkness when the Austin pulled up outside. Her husband was away, Lady Larmont told Mannering, and the servants long since in bed.

She opened the massive front door with her key, and stood aside for him to pass.

'After you,' murmured Mannering.

She went ahead, switching on a light before he entered. The hall was spacious and beautifully furnished, as one would have expected from so rich an owner.

She threw off her scarf, and walked with easy grace towards the stairs. He didn't trust her, but calculated that she was in too much danger to take chances with him. She led the way to a long narrow room on the first floor.

'Will you get me a drink?'

'What will you have?'

'Gin and vermouth.' She moved to an armchair and sank down.

He poured out two drinks and carried them across to her.

She raised her glass.

'To partnership,' murmured Mannering.

She looked tired and dispirited, and at the end of an adventure rather than at the beginning of one. Was she too young to stand up to much of what had happened tonight?

He glanced up at a photograph of Larmont; the man was in the fifties, and looked it.

'We're going to have a heart to heart talk, remember? As I don't want to deal with the police any more than you do, let's just find out if there is any way we can work together.'

'I don't trust you, I don't think you've told me the truth,' she said.

He shrugged, and she went on slowly: 'I'm an average human being in nearly every way, I wouldn't steal a penny from anyone if it weren't for one thing.' She gave a funny little laugh. 'I've a kink. That's why I married Larmont.'

She jumped up.

'Come over here,' she said.

She went to one of the book-cases, pressed a part of the carving, and it swung away from the wall. Behind was a combination wall safe. She knew the combination off by heart, twisted and turned, then opened it. She knew he was a thief, and yet took this chance. He watched her intently as her hand closed over a jewel-case. It was long and narrow and made of fine black leather. As she stood looking down at it, her eyes lost their heavy look of tiredness, taking on a glow which wasn't quite normal.

She opened the case slowly, and as the lid fell back, fire seemed to spring into the room. The light glinted on diamonds of such fiery brilliance that scintilla of a dozen different colours shot and sparked in front of Mannering's eyes.

He knew the love of jewels; he recognized it.

He felt a constriction at his chest as he looked at these, and had to force himself to remember that she might be trying to trick him. The fever in her eyes seemed to take on something of the brilliance of the diamonds. There was a necklace, two pendant ear-rings, two hair clips and two dress clips. These were the Moriarty diamonds, which had been on the market a year or so ago; the trade hadn't known who had bought them.

She fingered the jewels like a mother touching the cheek of her child. Her fingers caressed the glittering facets, moving lovingly from one to the other. He could hear her breathing like someone who had just finished a long and gruelling race.

She said: 'Do you see what my kink is?'

Mannering said quietly: 'Yes.'

'It is a disease. When I'm dealing with precious stones, I'm hardly sane.'

Mannering didn't speak.

She went on, her voice husky and uneven: 'I will lie, cheat, trick, rob—I will do anything, I tell you. Yet I never wear jewels. The compulsion to own them is so deep that I can't share it with anyone else. I hug it to myself like a guilty secret. Do you believe that?'

'I believe it,' Mannering said.

'They're meat and drink, flesh and blood, life and death to me.' She caught her breath. 'It's been the same ever since I can remember. I hadn't many when I was young, we weren't a wealthy family, but I gloated over the few I had, and envied everyone who had more. I would spend days gazing at private collections, I was known at every jewellers in London and Paris. I could seldom buy, but I had to see jewels, especially diamonds. *I couldn't help myself!*' She put out a hand and gripped his wrist. '*Do* you understand? It was like a fire burning inside me, I wanted more, more, more! I was like a miser, lusting for every diamond that I saw.'

'Then—I met Larmont.

'We were at a Paris jewel auction. There were certain stones he wanted, and he seemed to devour them with his eyes—just as I did. We were drawn together on that one mutual love—love! *Passion*.

'A few weeks later, we were married.

'I thought I had everything I wanted—that I could share everything with him, every stone he had. That I could travel the world looking for more, seeing every collection worth seeing, living for them. And, for a while, I was content.

'For a while,' she repeated. 'Just for a while.'

She moved to a chair and slumped down in it. He had never seen anyone more completely obsessed. When she had said that she would do anything to get possession of the jewels she coveted, she meant exactly that.

She opened her eyes and looked at him.

'Then I began to hate my husband,' she said. 'They were his jewels, not mine. I wanted them. I had to have diamonds which no one else could see, which I could hide from the world, I wanted beauty that was mine alone.'

The words poured out in a torrent, like water which had been dammed up for years.

'My husband had the same passion and owned jewels he would not let me see. I know that he buys secretly, so that no one can know what he possesses. I also know that he used Bryce, his solicitor, to buy collections and single stones. Not long ago I discovered that my husband didn't care one way or the other whether they were stolen or on the market legally; all he wanted was possession. I found out how to get into his strong-room. I knew where he put the keys and what precautions he took. I had the keys copied. One safe he never opened when I was with him, and one day when he was away, I went downstairs, and found the key in a safe in the strong-room. There I found jewels which I knew had been stolen.' After a moment's silence, she went on: 'I, too, would have done the same. Can you understand?'

'I think so,' Mannering said quietly.

She said: 'All that was six months ago. I knew then that I should never be happy unless I owned my own collection. I began to blackmail Bryce, and through him Morris, both of whom had bought stolen stones. They got jewels for me, diamonds mostly. I didn't care how they came by them. There was the Fesina collection.' She uttered the words softly, caressingly. 'My husband had half of it, including several pieces more beautiful than any I have ever seen. I wanted them above everything else, and—he *sold* them. I could have killed him. He sold them because he couldn't get the other half of the collection; but after they'd gone, the other half came into the market. They had been stolen in France, and imitations had been put in their place, so the theft hadn't been discovered. My husband was offered them by a French dealer and I've never seen him so furious. He sent for Bryce, and told Bryce to get the other jewels back, but—*I'd* told Bryce I wanted those Fesinas, that if I didn't get them, I would give him away to the police.'

'Bryce got them for me.'

She put her hand in the safe and drew out a case, opened it and stared down at the diamonds – those which Allen had stolen.

Mannering didn't speak.

She went on, and her first word made him jump.

'*Mannering* owned them. He's a dealer, and was injured when they were stolen. I didn't care, for I had the Fesinas, or half of them. The other half is still on the market, but at a fabulous price. I told Bryce what I wanted, but I knew I couldn't pay for the stones.'

Then he made a suggestion.

'He said he was finding a way to get hold of other jewels, from—a dealer, that he had a spy working for the dealer, and would stage a big robbery. He didn't tell me who the dealer was or who would do the work, but I wasn't satisfied with that, so I made him talk.

'He had used a young man named Allen to steal the Fesinas for me, and was using another young man, named Courtney, to plan the raid on the dealer. The plan is quite simple—I am to get my choice of what they steal, and they will sell the rest to my husband. Isn't it simple?'

She gave a strangled laugh.

Mannering murmured: 'So simple that it might work. So you knew that the first man they used was murdered, didn't you?'

She said: 'Now listen to me. You said you wanted a cut in big money, here *is* big money. Morris and Bryce won't be much use to me now. I will need someone else, who can break into a shop or open a safe. You're just right for that. What do you say?'

'What will Bryce and Morris say?'

'They don't know who I am, so they can't put the police on to me. In any case, they dare not do anything against me, because I can shop them.'

The word 'shop' sounded ugly on her lips.

'You would also have to shop your husband,' Mannering reminded her.

She stood up abruptly.

'Well, what are you waiting for?' She turned to face him. 'You will never have a better chance.'

Mannering said: 'This business about your husband—'

'Forget him,' she said. 'He doesn't matter, and in any case, he won't live long. I'll make sure of that. When he's dead, I will inherit—'

She never finished the sentence. A shot rang out, sharp, frightening. Mannering saw a man standing in the doorway with a smoking pistol in his hand.

It was Larmont.

His wife gave a little cough, and fell forward; there was a small hole in her forehead.

Chapter Nineteen

Larmont

Larmont did not move away from the door. His face was pale, but it was normal pallor. The most striking thing about him was his eyes. They had the same glitter as his wife's had shown a few minutes before.

'Don't move,' he ordered.

'How much did you hear?' Mannering asked.

'Everything. I was waiting for her,' Larmont said. 'I have known for some time that I couldn't trust her. Who are you?'

Mannering said: 'I'm a private detective, looking for a murderer.'

'Well, you've found one,' Larmont said. He laughed on a high-pitched note. 'I don't believe you, she wouldn't have offered you that share if you'd been a private detective.'

'She didn't know I was.'

Larmont shrugged. 'It doesn't matter. I can shoot you now and tell the police I heard a shot, came running to the scene and shot you as you were leaving. I'd be a hero for avenging my beautiful wife, wouldn't I?'

'The police would know the bullets came out of the same gun.'

'So they would. But supposing you left the gun by the body, meaning it to look like suicide?' He laughed, and raised his gun a few inches.

'You'd never get away with it.'

'I could try,' said Larmont. 'Turn round.'

Mannering didn't move.

'Turn round,' said Larmont, more sharply.

The shadow of death had never seemed nearer; Mannering knew that he was dealing with an abnormal man, and one whose guiding emotion now was fear.

'Turn—*round!*'

Mannering said: 'There's a fortune at Quinns. Mannering has some of the finest collections in the country. If your wife was right, why not get what you can of it? I can take the commonplace stuff, you can have the rare gems. I know a lot about Quinns.'

Larmont said slowly: 'I've never dealt with Mannering. I didn't think I could rely on him, he knows the police too well. Bryce should never have sold anything to him, but I couldn't get rid of half a collection at a good enough price, and he found Mannering would pay well.'

'It won't cost you a thing,' Mannering tempted. 'If this man Courtney really has a spy at Quinns, it should be easy. You need never pay for killing her, either.'

Larmont looked at his wife's dead body.

Mannering felt sweat gathering on his forehead.

There was horror here.

The woman who had been pulsing with life and loveliness was lying there, dead, and he could not forget her beauty. He had known her for a few hours. He had felt almost sorrow for her, knowing that she was not normal – yet her abnormality had given her a quality of evil, too. But for death to come with such awful suddenness – It might come to him; this very moment might be his last. The gun was pointing at his chest, and Larmont was only twenty feet away from him.

'No,' he said, slowly. 'It's too big a risk.'

'There needn't be any risk to you,' Mannering urged. 'We can move the body.'

'*What?*'

'We can take her away in my car. No one need ever know she was killed here. There's no danger for you.'

'The police aren't fools,' Larmont said. 'They'd come here as soon as they found the body. We can't clean blood off the carpet so that they'll find no trace. They're bound to discover where it happened, bound to. I've a great respect for the police. No, the only way is to shoot you and tell them you killed her.'

Mannering sweated. He saw that Larmont's finger was tightening on the trigger. There was a chance, only a chance, but he had to take it. He tensed himself to spring to the left.

The telephone bell rang.

Larmont, startled, glanced towards it. Mannering darted his right hand to his pocket, for the gun there. The telephone bell went on ringing. Larmont looked back at him. Mannering fired through his pocket, and hit him in the shoulder. Larmont swayed backwards. The bell kept ringing.

Mannering shot the gun out of his grasp.

As Larmont staggered against the wall, Mannering ran swiftly down the stairs, opened the front door and closed it behind him. The cold night air struck him viciously, but he had never accepted it so thankfully. Making his way to the Austin he saw that it was causing the attention of a peering policeman. This had to happen now; it had to happen when his heart was pounding and when there was a dead woman and a maddened man a few yards away.

He walked on, schooling his stride to one of unconcern. The policeman straightened up.

'Your car, sir?'

'Yes, officer.'

'I just wondered—there was a report of an Austin stolen this afternoon.'

Mannering forced a laugh.

'Not that one, I've had it for years.'

'Can you tell me what is in the dashboard pocket, sir?'

Mannering said: 'Yes, there's nothing very much. A half empty flat-fifty of Players Number 3, a wash-leather, some odd broken head lamp bulbs.

'Thank you, sir.' With maddening slowness the policeman opened the door and shone the flashlight on to the dashboard pocket. If the policeman was satisfied, he could get away safely, and garage the Austin. If the man wasn't satisfied, if he delayed Mannering even for five minutes, the damage would be done.

The light went off.

'That looks all right, sir.'

There was a cry from further along the square, a fight shone out from one of the houses; Larmont's house. The cry came again.

'Police! Police!'

The policeman said sharply: 'Here, what's this?'

Mannering hit him on the jaw, sent him flying, and sprang into the car.

Chapter Twenty

On The Run

Mannering reached the end of the square and swung into Oxford Street. He had five minutes grace, no more. The policeman would lose no time in getting to a telephone, his station would know about the Austin within that five minutes, and the patrol cars would be warned by radio.

He turned left, drove into a cul-de-sac and pulled up. Quickly, but without panic, he climbed out and hurried towards the Edgware Road.

He reached a small shop, which was in darkness. The single beam of a street lamp shone on a wig, and a display of cosmetics, in the window.

Mannering rang the bell; but there was no answer.

Old Sol, the owner, lived in a flat above the shop, and though used to the unconventional habits of theatrical folk, it was, after all, two o'clock in the morning.

Mannering glanced anxiously along the road; a police car was moving fast, probably in response to a message from the policeman at Grayling Square. He flattened himself against the door of the shop. The car flashed by, and the sound of the engine faded.

Mannering rang the bell again, and as he did so a light came on at the back of the shop.

With a screech of bolts, Old Sol opened the door.

'Such a time to wake an old man,' he grumbled. 'What is it, what is it?'

'I'm in a hurry, Sol,' Mannering said urgently.

'Mr. Mannering!'

'A real hurry,' Mannering :said and slipped into the shop.

Lorna stirred from sleep, as he opened the bedroom door. 'John, are you—?' She broke off.

He wore a suit which he had borrowed from Old Sol, who hired out clothes as well as wigs and cosmetics. All trace of make-up had gone, and except for his tired eyes, he looked normal enough.

Lorna shrugged her way into a dressing-gown and followed him into the sitting-room. 'Is everything all right?'

'Fairly all right.'

'Tell me.'

He told her. Half truths would not help, she would have to know, and there was the bond of absolute trust between them. He finished, at last.

'So it's started all over again,' she said bleakly. 'Fear of the police, being on the run from Bristow—oh, John.' There was a catch in her voice, and he could understand it only too well. She came across to him and he took her hands. 'Do you really feel safe?' she demanded.

'Unless Bryce talks. I don't know what Larmont will do. He will probably try to lie himself out of it. If Bristow *does* ask questions—'

Lorna said: 'He won't think you killed her, but he will know that you were there. There was a wonderful chance of being completely free from police suspicions, and it's gone.'

Mannering said: 'We'd better sleep on it, darling.'

Lorna moved away restlessly.

There was nothing he could do to reassure or comfort her. She had spent hours of anxious waiting, and the news had been worse than she'd dreamed.

She said suddenly: 'There wasn't anything of ours in the Austin, was there? The police will soon find it. If there were anything—'

'I bought the cigarettes weeks ago, we've both made sure that we've worn gloves whenever we've got into it. We've had it registered in the name of Reginald Brown for years, and garaged in the same lock-up garage. And don't forget the credit side. Bristow will probably find more stolen jewels at Larmont's than he's found in any one place for years, he'll be on top of the world. Larmont may tell his story but he'll break down under pressure. After all, Larmont did kill his wife.'

'If you go on like this,' said Lorna, 'you'll kill yours.'

The night hours dragged, and he couldn't sleep. He did not think Lorna was asleep, either. These were oppressive hours, and fear grew enormous with the darkness.

It had all the qualities of a nightmare.

The Austin might have been found by now. He wondered whether there could be anything in it which could lead to him.

Would Bristow have been called out?

Almost certainly, yes, as it was connected with precious stones; there wasn't anyone at the Yard who could touch Bristow at that.

If he went and told Bristow everything –

He said: 'Darling!'

She answered at once: 'Can't you sleep, either?'

'I've had a brainwave.'

'Forget it,' Lorna said.

'Supposing I tell Bristow everything, from the time I met Lady Larmont?'

Lorna sat up. 'Are you serious?' She put on the bedside lamp. 'Will you really do it?'

'Into the jaws of death,' said Mannering. 'I think it's the answer.' Sitting up, they stared at each other for what seemed an age. He could see no flaw in the idea, all he needed was a reasonable story of how he had met Lady Larmont. A simple story – that he had called on Bryce, returned to the car, and found her waiting for him.

He lifted the telephone and dialled Bristow's home number. He wasn't surprised to hear the sleepy voice of his wife.

'Why, no, he's been called out,' she said. 'I'm sorry, Mr. Mannering, but I don't know where he is. Can I give him a message?'

'I'll find him,' Mannering said, and as an afterthought, added: 'Just tell him that I rang up at—' he looked at the bedside clock – 'three-thirty-five, with a story to tell him about the Larmonts, will you?'

'I'll make a note of it,' promised Mrs. Bristow. 'Goodnight.'

Mannering replaced the receiver, and said: 'The boats are well and truly burned, my sweet. I hope we don't regret it.'

The front door bell rang.

Chapter Twenty-One

Fortune

Mannering put on his dressing-gown, slipped a gun into his pocket, and was at the door by the time the bell rang again. He didn't think that Bristow could have got here so soon, and in any case he was not likely to be as insistent as this.

He opened the door cautiously, his right hand about the gun. Anne Stafford almost fell inside. Her hair looked as if it had been in a hurricane, and her hands were blue with cold.

She was clutching a suitcase. Mannering took, it from her, surprised by its weight.

'Come for the night?' he asked.

'Oh, no! Please shut the door. He may have followed me.'

Mannering said sharply: 'Courtney?'

'Yes.'

Mannering switched off the light then stood listening for any sound of approach from the stairs. There was nowhere to hide up here, but a man could be in a doorway on the landings below.

He went down steadily, inspected the doorways and found each empty. He went to the next landing, and repeated the search; no one was there.

No one was in the hall, either.

He reached the street door, which was usually locked at night – but he must have forgotten to turn the key. *Had* he? The door must have been unlocked or the girl couldn't have entered, unless …

Could Anne be lying? Was this part of an act?

He stepped into the street and stood looking up and down, but saw no one. Satisfied, he bolted the door and went upstairs.

How had the girl got here at this hour, with that heavy suit-case? What had happened to make her so desperate? He remembered assuring Chittering that there was no need to worry about her integrity; had he been justified, or had he taken it for granted too easily?

There wasn't any time for a word with Lorna, and he didn't see that there was any need – the girl would tell Lorna exactly the same story as she would tell him.

'Was anyone there?' Anne asked.

She must have known there wasn't. Had she lost her nerve completely? There was something in this affair which almost scared him, he was prepared for it to go off at another tangent at any moment.

'I didn't see anyone,' he said lightly. 'What's it all about, Anne?'

'It was Courtney,' she said. 'He came to my house about an hour ago. He brought—that. He said I was to keep it and say nothing to anyone about it. He said I needn't worry about the money tomorrow, I needn't worry about anything, he had come into a fortune. When I asked questions, he changed his tune. He said that if I didn't keep the case at the house, he'd kill me. And—I think he meant it.'

She shivered.

'Well, well,' said Mannering. 'Shall we see what's in it?'

'It's locked.'

'I think we can deal with that,' said Mannering.

It didn't need an expert to force the locks. First one then the other clicked back. He lifted the case on to a chair, and opened it. He didn't know what he expected; certainly not to find it full of jewel cases.

There were fifty, at least. He took one out, and raised the lid.

Diamonds winked and glittered up at him.

He opened another: it contained emeralds.

Anne whispered: 'They must be—stolen.'

'That's right,' said Mannering, 'and I think I know where they were stolen from.' There was a pause. 'How did you get here?'

'I telephoned for a taxi. I just couldn't think of anything else to do. If you'd seen Courtney, you'd understand. He's frightened me before, but I've never been so frightened as I was tonight.'

She shivered.

'He just dumped these, and told you to look after them?'

'Yes. Yes!' she repeated.

If Courtney had stolen a fortune, would he take the chance of bringing it to Anne? It wasn't as unlikely as it might seem at first sight. Courtney would think that Anne was still willing to do everything he told her, that he still had that hold over her. Was there any other explanation?

'Mr. Mannering,' Anne said huskily, 'why are you looking at me like that?'

'I'm thinking,' said Mannering. 'Did Courtney say where he got these?'

'No.'

'What did he say?'

'He said that he'd come into a fortune, that it was a chance in a thousand and he'd taken it. I can't tell you anything else. When he threatened to kill me, I thought he was going to do it then. Look!' She pulled the sleeve of her coat back. There were angry red bruises on her forearm. 'He nearly broke my wrist,' she went on, 'Oh, I know it sounds crazy, but I do assure you I'm not really a neurotic little fool.'

'You did exactly the right thing,' Mannering assured her. 'Now sit down and relax, and I'll be back in a few minutes.'

He went into the kitchen where Lorna was making tea. The warmed pot was in her hand, and the kettle was singing. She looked good, with a dear, familiar loveliness. She wasn't likely to live through many nights more anxious than this.

He kissed the back of her neck. 'We have been presented with the great collection of jewels owned by Sir Lester Larmont, my sweet. Now what do you think of that?'

Chapter Twenty-Two

Bristow Wonders

Superintendent Bristow, looking as alert and unruffled as if he had not been called out of bed in the middle of the night, walked round the strong-room in the basement of the house in Grayling Square. It was five o'clock in the morning, Larmont was with him, nursing a bandaged wrist and shoulder.

So far he had given very little information. His butler had seen a man leaving by the back entrance, had gone down to the basement and found the strong-room door open and the safes empty; he'd rushed up to the street and shouted for the police.

A constable had been attacked by a man who had just walked from the house.

Bristow had reached the spot half-an-hour later.

He saw at once the strong-room and the safes had been opened by keys, either originals or duplicates. There was electric control, too, which had been switched off. The thief had walked in, used the keys, and hurried away; it could all have been done in half an hour.

The butler had been wakened by three 'loud reports'.

According to his story, Sir Lester was away for the night, and Lady Larmont had told him and the other servants that they need not stay up. As far as they knew, she hadn't returned.

All this, Bristow had discovered within ten minutes of entering the house. Then others arrived from the Yard and from the Division. He left men looking for clues in the strong-room, and went upstairs

– and the butler reported seeing a light under the door of Lady Larmont's sitting-room.

So someone had been there, during the disturbance.

Bristow had gone in –

Larmont had been sitting in an easy chair, nursing his wounds; and his dead wife had been on the floor, a few yards away from him.

Larmont had difficulty in talking, almost as if his power of speech was affected, but after a while he had told his story. He had come here and found a man threatening his wife, fired at the man, and hit his wife. He recited that in a flat, quivering voice, as if horror were shaking him.

The burglar had shot him in turn, and fled.

Larmont had staggered to the chair, dropped into it, and – he said – could not remember anything else. His mind had gone blank. All he could think about was his wife falling with the hole in her forehead. He was vague about the description of the man, said that as far as he remembered, it had all happened in a few seconds.

Bristow had taken him downstairs.

At first, he did not seem to realize what had happened there, and then suddenly he had pitched forward in a dead faint. A police-surgeon, called to examine the body of Lady Larmont, said that it was a simple case of shock, and that he ought to be allowed to rest. He had rested for an hour or more, then shown some signs of recovery, and insisted on going down to see the strong-room again.

Bristow watched him.

He walked from safe to safe, looking inside, pathetically hopeful, as if there was still a chance that the thief might have overlooked one case, or one tiny jewel. He seemed to have aged even while Bristow had been there, as if the double shock were more than he could stand.

The butler took him to his room, and a detective officer went with them.

Bristow returned to Lady Larmont's sitting-room, where the routine of investigation was in full swing. This had to be done, even though they had a 'confession' and the confession rang so true. The rest just didn't add up. One man had left by the back and the other by the front.

What had the second man been doing?

Had Larmont's wife returned, discovered what was happening, and been taken to her room and kept there until the job below was finished?

Bristow went back to the Yard, leaving a reliable man with Larmont. When he reached his office, he found a report of an incident at Ealing. The names Morris and Chittering caught his eye. He read on with tense interest. He still did not connect the Larmont affair with the one at Ealing until he saw the name of Bryce in the report.

Bryce – Larmont – *Mannering*!

He said aloud: 'He's behind it!'

The attack on the policeman at Grayling Square, the getaway in the Austin, all tied up with the way 'the Baron' had worked in the past.

Bristow said: 'If he's mixed up in this, I'll never trust him again.'

He jumped up, and hurried out of the office. As he reached the front hall, a sergeant on duty called out: 'Mr. Bristow! Telephone, sir.'

Bristow picked up the receiver, and said curtly: 'Bristow.'

'And this,' said Mannering, 'is Mannering.'

Bristow said with great deliberation: 'I am on my way to see you.'

'That's good,' said Mannering. 'I've a present for you. Oh, and you will be a wise man to put out a call for Mr. William Courtney, of—'

He gave Courtney's address.

'Why?' demanded Bristow.

'He stole the Larmont jewels tonight, as far as I can make out'

'Just you wait in for me!' cried Bristow.

He hurried to his car, reaching Green Street just after half-past five.

Mannering drew him into the flat.

'A bargain is a bargain and I think you'll find this one worth your trouble.' He led the way to the study, and as he opened the door, asked. 'Did you get my message?'

'What message?'

'I telephoned you about half-past three. Your wife promised to tell you as soon as you got back. Or haven't you been home yet?'

'No.'

'It will catch up.' said Mannering.

Several of the cases from the Larmont collection were on his desk, and suddenly he opened one; it was as if light and fire had leapt into the room. Bristow caught his breath. Mannering smiled, opened another, and withdrew a necklace like a cascade of diamonds.

'Not bad, is it?' The stones shimmered through his fingers. 'I haven't examined them all, but I fancy you'll find everything taken from Larmont's place. Have you been there yet?'

'Yes,' said Bristow.

According to Larmont, a man had been at the house with his wife – and if Bristow's reasoning were right, that man had been Mannering.

Bristow tried not to think.

'What does Larmont say?' asked Mannering.

'Have you seen him?'

'Oh, yes.'

Bristow said slowly; 'I hope you aren't trying to fool me, because the situation has grown too serious for that.'

Mannering told the story as he had planned with Lorna, making up only the part about meeting Lady Iris by appointment. He left nothing else out, and realized that this was the first time since they had known each other that he had told a story so forthright.

He finished mildly enough: 'And after I'd left the house all I could think of was getting away. When I'd had time to think over it, and talk it over with Lorna—' he shrugged. 'That's why I telephoned your flat.'

'What time was that?'

'About half-past three.'

'What time did the girl get here?'

'Soon afterwards,' said Mannering.

'Is she still here?'

'In the sitting-room, with Lorna. The only thing puzzling me is that Courtney chose tonight to make his raid, and got away with that lot. It's almost as if someone opened the doors for him.'

Bristow said: 'Prepared to go into the witness box and testify against Larmont?'

'Yes.'

'Admitting that you were disguised?'

'Why not? I was trying to get to the bottom of my own problem, and didn't want Lady Larmont to recognize me. That is all straight and above board.'

'Oh, yes,' said Bristow. 'I'm beginning to believe in miracles.' He chuckled, unexpectedly. 'What happened at Ealing tonight?'

Chapter Twenty-Three

New Leaf

Mannering lit a cigarette, outwardly at ease, inwardly anxious.

If he told the truth, he would virtually be in Bristow's power.

The years of liking between them had always been marred by that feeling of distrust – Mannering's for any policeman, Bristow's for anyone who had been a thief. Was this really the turning point? Mannering tried to see the situation as Bristow would. When he knew what Mannering had been doing, would the policeman or the man come out uppermost?

'Make up your mind,' Bristow said.

'I hope you're playing fair,' said Mannering. 'This is all off the record.'

'Why do you think I've come by myself, if I'm trying to get a statement to use against you?' asked Bristow. 'I'm not carrying a pocket dictaphone.'

Mannering forced a laugh. 'Well, here goes—'

He talked freely, leaving nothing out.

Bristow sat back in the armchair, drawing deeply on his cigarette. His face was blank, it was impossible to judge his thoughts. Mannering didn't try.

Bristow, watching Mannering closely, needed little convincing that he was hearing the truth at last. Many and many a time he had crossed swords with the Baron, trying to trick him into making an admission; and always he had failed. He knew this was partly because his heart was not entirely in it. He had sympathy for Mannering, both because he liked him, and because he thought he could gain results in the field of crime where, for various reasons, the police could not.

Take this case.

Ordinary police methods had got him nowhere. Mannering's methods had slashed through routine and red tape and uncovered most of the truth – perhaps all of it. Any man who had the nerve to do what Mannering had done deserved to get away with it. Practically everyone at the Yard would scream blue murder if they even suspected what was in his mind, but –

Would there be much difficulty in getting evidence against Bryce, Morris and Courtney? There was no proof yet as to who had killed Reginald Allen, but that was almost incidental, to the new situation. Mannering had come up against a cunning plot, the full ramifications of which were not yet known, and broken it in a few days.

What should he, Bristow, do? As a man he had no doubt, but as a policeman – that was different.

Mannering finished his story.

He wished he knew what Bristow was thinking, wished he wasn't so poker-faced. His own feelings were mixed. He had severed all links with the Baron of the past, had come right out. He could only hope desperately that he would not live to regret it.

He said: 'Now what, Bill?'

Bristow said: 'Thank you, John. You won't regret any of it. Now, about Morris and Bryce—'

Lorna came in, half an hour afterwards, with a tea-tray,

'I can run to breakfast, if you're ready for it.'

'No thanks, Lorna!' Bristow was bright and brisk. 'I must get back to the Yard, I'm afraid. How much have you to do with all this?'

'All this what?'

'This turning of the leaf?'

She said primly: 'You do take sugar, don't you?'

Bristow sat back and roared with laughter.

It was half-past six when the door closed on him. Mannering's eyes danced as he stretched out his arms.

'I think it's worked.'

'You told him?'

'Yes, I told him. Believe in miracles?'

Lorna didn't speak, but Mannering watched the tears that glistened in her eyes, realized, perhaps more vividly than he had yet done, how desperate she had felt about the struggle which had gone on between him and the police. Quite suddenly, he pulled her close and kissed her.

After a while Mannering went on: 'Bristow is now having both Morris and Bryce watched, he telephoned the Yard ten minutes ago. He isn't going to do anything about either of them yet, but will wait until he sees what they get up to when they hear of the death of Lady Larmont. He's going to release that story to the Press as if he doesn't know that Larmont shot her. I told him I doubted the sense of that move, but he's stubborn.'

Lorna didn't speak.

'He's putting out a general call for Courtney, and will pick him up the moment he can,' Mannering added. Then: 'How is Anne?'

'Sleeping,' said Lorna. 'She'll be all right. And darling, I'm sure she's quite honest. I could tell that you were doubtful. You needn't be.'

'I hope not.'

'What makes you doubt her?' asked Lorna.

'The oddness of it all. But it's nonsense, she wouldn't have brought that case-load of stuff here if she hadn't been on the level. Blame my suspicious mind!' Mannering laughed. 'If things go well, Bristow will pick up Courtney in the next hour or two, and we'll have the explanation of that particular mystery.'

'Mystery?'

'Well, either that, or a coincidence so big I just can't believe in it. At the very time I was talking to Lady Larmont and while her husband was listening, Courtney was downstairs among the jewels. What a time to choose? He told Anne he'd had a tremendous slice of luck. What was it? That he happened to pay a social call and walked in, found the keys outside the strong-room and helped himself? Not on your life.'

'I suppose not,' said Lorna.

'Far, far too perfect a set-up for coincidence,' Mannering went on. 'Someone knew there would be trouble between Larmont and his wife. He may have suspected that I would be about, and chosen that very time for the raid. It must have been someone who had access to the strong-room and the keys. Now Lady Larmont told me that she had a spare set made—remember? I think she forgot to add the spicy bit.'

Lorna put down her cup.

'I know I'm dense, darling, but I still don't see it.'

'Look at it this way. Lady Larmont did not know that Bryce had realized who she was. But Bryce knew, and probably gave Larmont a hint, making pretty sure of a showdown. If Bryce knew what she was up to, he may have had a shrewd idea that she was going to stage a raid on the strong-room. If he managed to get hold of her set of keys and send them over to Courtney, Courtney would have been all ready for his raid. It was unexpected—a slice of luck, remember? Morris was in it, too—that's why they fell for the fake message so easily.'

'I suppose you're right, but I thought they were working on Quinns, through Anne.'

'Quinns would be twice as dangerous and only about a quarter as profitable—a second line of attack. And what is more, Bryce didn't discover the identity of the woman who was blackmailing him until after he'd laid on everything for Quinns. It would be easy enough to switch attacks. The weakness of the whole thing came when the police were called in tonight. Bryce daren't take over the jewels, and Morris couldn't—they were both too likely to be watched and questioned. That left Courtney in a spot. I can imagine he finished the job, contacted Bryce, and they had to find a temporary hiding place for the jewels. Anne, already in their hands, was the answer.'

'I suppose it could be like that,' Lorna said.

'Still doubtful?'

'I don't know. I'm so tired I'm almost past thinking and what brain I have is used up in giving thanks that you and Bristow are to work together, and everything is to be happy ever after.'

She kissed him.

Courtney woke, just after nine o'clock, and looked round an unfamiliar room. After leaving the suitcase at Conroy Street, he had gone on to a third-rate hotel in Paddington on the chance that his own flat would be raided by the police. No-one had asked any questions, he hadn't even been invited to sign the register.

As he viewed the ugly room, his smile was the smile of a well-satisfied man.

After ten minutes, he rang the bell. A young maid answered promptly. She looked fresh and pleasant, and spoke with a marked foreign accent. When she brought in tea, he managed to touch her arm, as if accidentally, and she smiled at him coyly. In a couple of days, she would be a pushover. He sipped his tea and forgot her, because he was dazzled by jewels. He hadn't time to enjoy them the night before, being too busy getting the stuff out of the strong-room.

Thanks to Bryce! Bryce had laid it all on, by-passing Morris.

There was a good joke about that. Bryce still thought he was at his own rooms. Bryce would have a shock when he discovered he was missing.

Courtney frowned suddenly.

It was one thing to have a fortune in precious stones, another to get rid of it. Bryce would look after the selling but it was a pity he had to leave it to him. If he could cash-in himself –

He couldn't, because he didn't know the markets.

He had Bryce where he wanted him. Five thousand, and he'd take a chance – but he'd have enough on both Bryce and Morris to make sure that they didn't cheat him out of his share.

He had been instructed to take the jewels to Bryce, but at the last moment Bryce had told him, by telephone, to hold them. He wondered why.

The one thing that didn't occur to him was that Anne would fail him.

He didn't trouble to shave, but dressed and went down to the telephone. He dialled Bryce's office number, but Bryce hadn't yet arrived, so he dialled the Hampstead house. Bryce, himself, answered; his voice was taut with fury.

'Where the hell have you been?'

'Playing safe,' said Courtney, airily. 'Everything's all right, you don't have to worry.'

'Where are you?'

'Never mind. Where can I meet you?'

Bryce said: 'You can't. We had some trouble last night, and the police might be watching me. Where's the parcel?'

'It's quite safe.'

'*Where is it?*'

Courtney said: 'A friend of mine is looking after it. What's this about the police?'

'Remember you had a visitor the other night?'

Courtney caught his breath.

'Morris and I had one last night,' said Bryce. 'We've got to lie low, because the police caught up on the visitor. Tell me where the stuff is, and I'll make arrangements to have it collected.'

'Not on your life,' said Courtney.

He hung up, and stared at the pencilled marks on the wall near the telephone. But he didn't see them. Bryce and Morris were in trouble, and they didn't know where the jewels were.

He had a fortune on his hands, and did not know how to dispose of it.

He put two more pennies in, and dialled Quinns' number; Peters answered him.

'May I speak to Miss Staffer, please? This is a personal call.'

'I'm sorry,' said Peters, 'but Miss Staffer isn't in this morning.'

Courtney hung up, and stared at the wall. He didn't feel at all good. He hadn't given serious thought to the possibility that Anne would be unreliable. She didn't know what was in the suit-case. She might guess there were stolen goods, but she couldn't know.

Or – had she forced the lock and looked?

Why hadn't she gone to work?

Courtney hurried up to his room, flung on a coat, and went out. He stopped at a news-stand to buy a paper, then hailed a passing taxi.

'Sloane Square,' he said, and settled back in the cab.

He unfolded the paper.

Headlines about Lady Larmont's death shrieked up at him. There was the bare announcement that she had been shot, nothing about Larmont's statement. There was also a screaming headline about the robbery. No one reading the account could miss the implication – that the thief had killed Lady Larmont.

Courtney felt icy cold.

When the coldness thawed, he began to feel frightened.

Chapter Twenty-Four

Frightened Man

Courtney left the cab near Sloane Square station, and went across to another news-stand and bought more papers. Then he went to a cafe, ordered eggs and sausages and tea, because fear seemed to make him hollow in the stomach, and glanced avidly through each of the newspapers. They all had the same story and carried the same implication – that the thief had killed Lady Larmont.

He felt perspiration break out on his forehead.

He started to eat, and discovered that he wasn't hungry after all.

He left the cafe, schooling himself to walk with a slow and leisurely stride. If he hurried, he might attract attention and that was the last thing he wanted to do. As he neared Anne's turning, he turned up the collar of his coat, in an instinctive attempt at some sort of disguise.

Then he told himself that no one could possibly know that he had been at Grayling Square.

Couldn't they?

Bryce and Morris had obviously been questioned by the police. Bryce hadn't talked, but Morris – he didn't trust Morris. He could imagine the man's sallow face and odd-shaped eyes; a furtive swine.

Crazy! Morris wouldn't dare.

The fear remained.

He saw a man standing at the corner of Conroy Street. He was just the type Courtney had always imagined a plainclothes detective would be. Courtney moistened his lips, squared his shoulders and walked past the end of the street. He glanced along it casually, and saw another man, very similar to the first one, at the far end.

Courtney walked on.

Had the men been watching Anne's flat?

Where was she?

Could she have gone to the police?

He reached a telephone kiosk, hesitated, then dialled the number of a friend.

'Jerry?' asked Courtney, abruptly.

'Sure, who's that?'

'Bill Courtney.'

'Hiya, Bill! How's tricks?'

'You can earn yourself a fiver.'

'Just tell me how!'

'Meet me at Sloane Square station, as soon as you can.'

'Suits me, all right.'

Courtney rang off, and walked towards the station. He was ten minutes ahead of Jerry, a tall, fair-haired youth, who came ambling along, smoking a *Camel*.

He listened.

'Gimme the money first,' he said.

Courtney waited at a cafe near Victoria Station, and the time dragged. He'd left Jerry at eleven o'clock, and it was now half-past twelve. He had been almost alone in the cafe at first, now it was crowded, the lunch hour rush was on.

The manageress asked him if he would make room for another customer, and he paid his bill and went outside. It was beginning to rain. Wherever he looked, he seemed to see policemen, but they took no notice of him. He couldn't go far from the cafe, or he would miss Jerry.

Had Jerry taken his money, and then run out on him?

He heard a clock strike one.

He smoked three cigarettes in quick succession. What would he not give for a drink! But if he were to nip down into a pub, he might miss the other man. He strolled up and down, and now he was sure that one of the policemen was interested in him.

If Anne had squealed –

He would kill her.

He turned – and saw Jerry, hurrying along. There was nothing ambling about Jerry's gait now, and he looked tense and alarmed. They met outside the cafe.

'What's happened?'

'Come on, I want a drink.' They crossed the road to a public house, and ordered two double whiskies.

'What *happened?*' demanded Courtney hoarsely.

'You're asking me! As soon as I rang the bell, a couple of bulls come up. They asked me a hundred questions—did I know Anne well, did I know you, why had I called to see her? They let me go at last, but I was hanging around for an hour or more. And—they followed me.'

Courtney gulped down his whisky.

'I gave them the slip,' Jerry boasted, and wiped his forehead. 'What job have you been doing?'

'I haven't done a job!'

'That so?' Jerry sneered. 'Okay, okay, you don't have to tell me, only I don't want any more errands like that one. Wouldn't go through that again for ten quid.'

'Are you sure you gave them the slip?'

'Sure? You're talking to Jerry Ryden, son!'

Courtney said: 'Yes—yes, thanks, Jerry.'

'Can't stay any longer, pal, I've gotta date.'

He went off.

Courtney left the pub, and caught the first bus to come along. The fact that Anne's house was being watched told him everything he wanted to know, and the fact that the police had asked whether Jerry knew Courtney was proof that she'd squealed.

The police had those diamonds.

And – it was a murder rap.

Was Bryce behind this? Bryce wouldn't have put the police on to Anne, but had Bryce killed the woman?

He wouldn't be surprised.

Nothing would surprise him, now.

He had had a fortune in his hands; it was gone; and he was wanted for murder. He couldn't get away from those facts. Supposing Bryce had got him to do the dirty work, planning to collect the jewels and frame him for the murder? No, Bryce wouldn't have done that, it wasn't reasonable, he had too much on Bryce.

Morris?

No, he decided, each man had too much to lose. He was filled with an insensate fury against Anne. It was her fault. If she'd kept her mouth shut, there would have been nothing to worry about.

He heard the conductor call: 'All change,' and saw with some surprise that he was at Shepherd's Bush. It was drizzling with rain and there were people about. A newsboy stood in a doorway. Courtney went across and bought an *Evening News*.

The murder and the robbery had the front page headlines, and there was a sub-heading:

POLICE SEEK YOUTH

The police are anxious to interview a youth named "William Courtney, of 79 Linden Road, who they think may be able to give them valuable information about the robbery at Sir Lester Larmont's house in Grayling Square. Courtney is described as –

It was a good description.

It didn't say that he was wanted for murder, but he knew exactly what it meant.

His mouth was dry.

He needed money.

He couldn't stay in London.

He went to a telephone kiosk and dialled Bryce's office. He didn't give his name to the girl who answered, and tried to disguise his voice. It was some time before Bryce came on the line.

'Yes, who is that?'

'No names,' Courtney said in his normal speaking voice.

'Just a minute.' There was silence again, and a wild thought went through Courtney's mind, that Bryce was sending a message to the police, that the call would be traced. But the police couldn't trace calls on the automatic system, could they?

A middle-aged woman walked past the box, and then past again, staring at him.

Bryce said: 'All safe, now, I had to get rid of someone who was with me. What the hell did you do last night?'

'I didn't kill—'

'Shut up!'

Courtney licked his lips,

'Where are you?' Bryce asked.

'I'm at Shepherd's Bush.'

'And the stuff?'

Courtney didn't answer.

Bryce said: 'Listen, Courtney, that stuff is so hot it will burn anyone who gets near it. Have you got it well hidden?'

Courtney said: 'My friend let me down. She—she tipped off the police.'

There was another silence; a long silence; then Bryce spoke again in a very different voice, smoother and friendlier, as if the tension had gone.

'Okay, Courtney, that can't be helped, it's always the same when you trust a woman. Meet me at the Windmill, Wimbledon Common, at four o'clock. We've got to talk this thing out.'

Courtney said: 'Sure, I'll be there. But I didn't—'

'Of course you didn't,' said Bryce, 'we'll see you through. Don't worry. Four o'clock.'

'Thanks,' said Courtney. 'Thanks.'

He rang off.

The woman was still pacing up and down, and glaring at him.

Courtney walked to the bus stop, trying to think. Why should Bryce want to see him on Wimbledon Common?

Why go so far out of town?

Bryce wouldn't want to see him anywhere near his office or his house, of course, nor near Morris's place; but Bryce had offered to help, and that meant money. A ticket out of the country too, perhaps.

He couldn't guess.

The more he thought of it, the less he felt that he could trust Bryce or Morris. When he looked at it squarely, he knew that he had a lot on them. True Morris knew he'd killed Allen, but Morris had been in that, too. If the police caught him and he told the whole story, they would be finished – each would spend a long time in jail. If he were in their shoes, what would he do?

He would want himself out of the way.

Wimbledon Common was a big, desolate patch of country in the winter, and he knew that the Windmill, a pleasure spot in summer, was a long way from the main roads and from people – *why arrange to meet him there?*

It would be getting dark at four o'clock. The more he thought of it, the less he liked it.

He had to see Bryce; but he wouldn't take any chances. He caught a bus, and it was empty on top, and he took out his automatic; it was filled with seven bullets. He had plenty and to spare if there were any emergency.

He didn't trust Bryce.

He didn't trust anyone.

He had a special corner in hatred for Anne Staffer.

Chapter Twenty-Five

Rendezvous

When Mannering saw Anne just before one o'clock that day, she looked as if a great burden had been lifted off her shoulders.

'Troubles nearly over,' he said, cheerfully.

'I can't tell you how *grateful* I am to you,' she told him a little tremulously. 'It will be all right if I go to the shop this afternoon, won't it?'

'I don't see why not. If you'd prefer to stay here, you can, you know.'

'I'd rather be working.'

'Right. Come back here tonight, though, unless the police have caught Courtney.'

She said: 'You're both so good,' and, as she left the room, the front door bell rang. A moment later Mannering heard Chittering's voice, saying: 'Lorna, my sweet, you're looking lovelier than ever, which means that John didn't break his neck last night.'

'He's waiting until another night,' said Lorna. 'You're just in time for lunch.'

Chittering smiled gratefully, and stuck his head through the study door.

''lo John. I suppose you've heard all about my sad story of last night?' He grinned shamefacedly, 'The first thing I knew about it was a clout over the head.'

He touched his head gingerly.

'Do you know who hit you?'

'Don't tell me you do.'

Mannering launched into a fairly detailed description of what had happened.

Chittering groaned. 'Why do stories like this *always* have to be off the record?' He sipped his drink. 'You had quite a night out, didn't you? Did you release the Courtney story?'

'Yes.'

'Hum. That accounts for Bristow's amiability. All to the good, I suppose, although I used to enjoy the sparks that flew when you two met. Er—is it all right for Anne to stay here until they've picked Courtney up?'

'Of course.'

'Thanks. I'm more relieved than I can say. There was something in the way that devil talked to Anne—that reminds me—do you think Bristow was wise to let the Press know he's after Courtney?'

Mannering shrugged.

'Meaning you don't. It wouldn't surprise me if Courtney gives trouble before they catch him, that's why I'm anxious Anne shouldn't be wandering about on her own. A clear case of murder, I take it?'

Mannering said evasively, 'I think there's a lot Bristow hasn't told us.'

They lunched; happily and gaily as far as Anne and Chittering were concerned. Afterwards he took her to the shop.

Mannering drove to Scotland Yard.

He was greeted almost expansively by Bristow.

'Come in, John. Sit down. Cigarette?'

Mannering lit up.

'This feels just like home.'

'Let's keep it that way,' said Bristow. 'I've had a word with the Assistant Commissioner off the record. He's always been half-way in your favour, and he's quite agreeable to a kind of unofficial link. Keep within reasonable bounds, and we'll be able to work together a lot.'

'So the impossible happens! What about Courtney?'

'We haven't picked him up yet.' Bristow frowned. 'We've searched his fiat, and know he has a gun. I'm not at all happy about him. I've had the girl watched—she was followed with Chittering to Quinns. I'm having Quinns watched, too, just in case Courtney makes trouble.'

'What about Bryce and Morris?'

'I haven't touched Bryce yet, but I'm having him followed. Also Morris. Larmont is suffering from shock, and will be flat out for two or three days, perhaps longer. We found some records at Grayling Square, listing all the stuff he had there. Several stolen collections were in that strong-room, and we've identified them from the stuff you presented to us. Larmont worked with Bryce, we've plenty of evidence about that, and of course Bryce worked with Morris.'

'Why not pick them up?' asked Mannering.

Bristow said: 'They were going to raid your place, I think, and switched off on to Larmont's when the chance offered. They wouldn't have raided Quinns if they hadn't been sure they could dispose of the stuff. I want to tab Bryce and Morris and find out if they lead to anyone else—there may be someone behind it we know nothing about yet. I'd like to make a clean sweep. And that reminds me—' His voice assumed an almost unnatural innocence – 'you know more of the undercover buyers of jewels than anyone else in the country. Will you try to find out who Bryce sold to, as well as Larmont?'

Mannering chuckled. 'If you think I can help—'

'I know you can. '

'Let's get Courtney first,' said Mannering.

Courtney left the bus within a few hundred yards of the Windmill on Wimbledon Common. It was twenty-five minutes to four, and already the light was fading. The drizzle left a beading of moisture on his coat, but the hand holding the gun in his empty pocket was warm and sticky.

He took up a position near the deserted tea rooms, but at five to four, there was still no sign of Bryce. Peering from the cover of a thicket of bushes he watched a motorcycle wobbling across the Common.

The rider stopped a few yards away, and looked around him. He propped up the machine on its stand, and then stepped nearer the Windmill.

The man took something from his pocket.

Courtney craned his neck.

It was a gun.

Courtney felt a shiver run up and down his spine. He took out his own gun, and stepped forward.

The man spun round.

'Keep your hands in sight,' Courtney ordered.

The motor-cyclist was a little man, with a red face on which the moisture clung lingeringly. His small eyes were frightened, and he backed a pace.

'Looking for me?' asked Courtney.

The man licked his lips.

'Yes—yes, Bryce sent a message, he—'

'There's no need to prevaricate, I saw the gun. What's the message?'

'He—he said—'

'He told you to bump me off. Is that it?'

The motor-cyclist swallowed, then said hoarsely: 'Listen, I only work for Bryce! Surely we can—'

Courtney shot him. It needed only one bullet, and the man fell. Courtney stood quite still, with the smoking gun in his hand, staring at the Windmill; was anyone there? Silence settled round him, the only sound the echo of the shot.

The motor-cyclist had eleven pounds in his wallet. Courtney pocketed this, and also the gun. Then he dragged the body beneath the bushes.

There was blood on his hands when he had finished.

He wiped it off on the grass, and went to the motorcycle. It was a modern one, fast and powerful. He started the engine, heading for the road. He was filled with a seething fury, against Bryce and against Morris. He didn't care what he did, provided he *killed*.

They would get him for murder, he felt sure of that – and they might as well get him for something he had done thoroughly.

He drove fast but skilfully, with a gun in each pocket of his overcoat, laughing as he went.

He was lucky.

Bryce left his office just after five o'clock. It was in a narrow turning in Lincoln's Inn. The misty night made it difficult to see anyone clearly, but Courtney recognized Bryce in the light of a lamp outside the building.

He shot him, twice.

He saw another man, standing nearby, rush forward; he didn't know it was a Yard man. He fired and hit the man in the chest. The sound of the shots was still echoing when he started off on the motor-bicycle. There could be no immediate pursuit, he would have several minutes grace before the cry of 'murder' was raised.

He wondered vaguely who the second man had been.

He drove along Oxford Street in the thick of the rush-hour, negotiating the traffic mechanically. They would know who had shot Bryce, of course – or they would guess. They would probably expect him to go for Morris and Anne. He couldn't go to Anne's house, because he knew they were on the watch there, but they might not be watching at Quinns.

There was a risk in keeping the motor-cycle, but he had taken pretty well every risk a man could take, one more or less would make no matter.

He wanted to kill Anne.

He couldn't think beyond that.

But he was cunning.

If she'd told the police about the suit-case, she had almost certainly told them where he had waited for her so often; so they would be on the look-out at that spot. To go there would be to ask for trouble. But – could he follow her?

Would she be followed by the police?

He realized the danger was acute, but Hart Row drew him like a magnet. He parked the motor-cycle, and walked a little way along Bond Street. From there he could see Hart Row.

He looked at his watch repeatedly; no one would be surprised if a man was kept waiting by his girl friend.

He grinned.

Then he saw a Lagonda nose its way out of Hart Row. There was a man at the wheel, and a girl next to him. He knew the man – Mannering.

He recognized Anne.

The car swung right, and passed him. His hand tightened about the gun in his pocket, but he didn't shoot, he knew that he would probably miss. Where was she going with Mannering. Home?

He hurried back to the motor-cycle, and was on the move in a matter of seconds. Sighting the Lagonda near Hyde Park Corner, he roared past it towards Victoria, then pulled in at the side of the road. It passed, and he saw that it was heading towards Sloane Square.

Was Mannering taking her home?

He drove along towards Fulham, parked the motor-cycle, and walked across to a telephone kiosk. Carefully he checked Mannering's address – 21c, Green Street, Chelsea.

So it looked as if Anne had gone home with him.

Courtney didn't go back to the motor-cycle. It had served its purpose, and was now only an added danger. His eye was caught by a two-seater coupe. He strolled towards it. By a stroke of tremendous luck, the door wasn't locked.

He got into the driving seat. The key wasn't in the ignition, and he tried several that he had on his own chain; they were all too big.

It wasn't so easy after all, his fingers wouldn't keep steady.

Time was all important.

Then he heard footsteps, and a man drew near. Courtney took out his gun.

The footsteps slowed down, and a hand touched the door. Courtney flung it open savagely, sending the man staggering back. He jumped out, and smashed his fists into the man's face.

Something fell with a light rattle, on to the pavement.

Courtney groped on the ground for the keys; his luck held, and he found them. The engine started at a touch.

Coming up to the Lagonda, he saw that it was parked outside a house.

Another car was parked further along the street, and there was a man at the wheel. There wasn't much doubt that the police were watching.

His mind was filled with the one thought of vengeance. Beyond that he hardly cared.

He walked along the next street and found that there was a waste patch of land between Mannering's and several other houses. It was very dark, and he saw no signs of a watch being kept.

There was a fence at the back of a building. Courtney climbed over without difficulty, and found himself in a long, narrow garden.

He went nearer – and caught his breath.

There was a piece of iron jutting out near a drain pipe – when he stood close to the house he could look upwards and just see it; and others higher up. It was like a do-it-yourself fire-escape, and would make climbing easy.

He took off his coat, put the guns into his jacket pocket, and started to climb.

Chapter Twenty-Six

Baron's Way

Mannering had been in the flat for ten minutes, and was looking through some letters which had come by the last post, when the telephone bell rang.

He lifted the receiver. 'Hallo.'

'John?'

'Hallo, Bill.'

Bristow said: 'John, listen. Courtney is on the rampage. He was waiting for Bryce outside his office this evening, and shot him through the head and chest. He's dead. He also shot the man we had watching Bryce. We've doubled the watch at Morris's place, and I'm doubling it at yours.'

'Thanks, Bill,' Mannering said quietly.

'She's there with you, isn't she?'

'Yes.'

'I'll have everyone who calls at your place screened,' Bristow went on. 'Just keep the girl indoors until you get the all clear.'

Mannering put the receiver down, and glanced at the door. There wasn't any need to tell Anne or Lorna about this yet. Chittering would probably know, but he would have the sense not to cause alarm.

The telephone bell rang again.

'John?' It was Chittering, alert, anxious. 'Look after Anne as if she were gold. Courtney's berserk. He's killed Bryce, nearly killed one of Bristow's men and is working up to anything. I'm assigned to the job. Tell Anne I can't make it at seven, and for the love of Mike, keep her there until they catch Courtney.'

'Don't worry, old chap.'

Chittering said: 'John, just between you and me, I'd swing for anyone who hurt that girl.'

He rang off.

Mannering put back the receiver with mixed feelings. The case which had started with violence was ending in violence – and all he could do was to sit back and wait until there was news from Bristow.

Ought he to have come to terms with Bristow?

If he had been working as in the past, he would have held that suit-case, would have tried to sell Courtney a dummy – and that would probably have come off.

There was a further mistake Bristow had made – he had released the statement that the police wanted to question Courtney.

He couldn't blame Bristow. If the police had withheld the name and Courtney had gone wild, there would have been censure from all quarters.

Lorna looked in.

'Busy, darling? Do you know when Chittering is coming for Anne?'

'Sorry, I forgot to tell you—he's out on a job. Can we manage?'

'Of course, I'll tell Ethel.' Lorna went into the kitchen, leaving the door ajar. Mannering heard Ethel say: 'I'll lay the extra place this minute, Ma'am.'

'I should open a window,' Lorna said. 'It's so steamed up in here.'

Mannering heard a window going up – and his lips twisted wryly. That window led to the iron rungs rammed into the wall, and which he and Lorna had come to call the Baron's Way. When he needed to get out, or in, without the police knowing, he'd used those iron rungs. Some of them had been placed there when a fire escape had been mooted, and then for some reason, not finished. He had put others in himself.

Mannering heard Lorna chatting to Anne, and then the closing of the sitting-room door after they had both gone.

Courtney was near the top of the house when he saw a woman appear at the window, her arms stretched up. She couldn't see him unless she leaned out, but for a moment he was afraid she was going to. He slid his free hand towards his pocket.

The window was opened a few inches.

Courtney stretched up, clutching another rung.

He didn't think of falling, had no fear.

He hauled himself up again, and could see through the kitchen to an open door. He steadied himself on the rungs, and pushed the window farther up – it ran easily, making little noise.

He squeezed himself through, with a hand at his pocket, but there was no need for alarm. He stepped over the sink and on to the floor.

There was a sound of rattling cutlery, not far off; that was all.

He took out his own gun, keeping the motor-cyclist's in reserve, and stepped towards the door. Through it he saw the maid laying the table. Several other doors leading off the hall were closed. He stepped softly towards the nearest, which was ajar – and caught a glimpse of a man's hand, resting on a desk.

Mannering's.

He looked down, and saw that the key was in the lock of the door. He closed it, softly, and turned the key. That caused a click.

He glanced round.

The maid was coming out of the dining-room, and saw him. She opened her mouth wide, and flung up her hands. He fired at her. She fell screaming. He heard a shout from the room in which he had locked Mannering, and an exclamation from another room. The door opened. A woman he didn't know appeared, and behind her, he glimpsed Anne.

'Why this is fine,' he said hoarsely. 'I've just come to say hallo, Anne.'

Mannering heard the click as his door closed, and then heard another sound – of the key turning in the lock. He leapt up, and as he did so, heard a scream and a shot. The shot sounded deafening through the locked door. He rushed towards it, then stopped.

The door wasn't only locked, it was almost burglar-proof.

Mannering felt his pulse racing, forced himself to steady, to think. He picked up the telephone and dialled 999. A girl answered. 'Tell the police to come to 21c Green Street, Chelsea—say Courtney is here.' He didn't wait for an answer but pulled open his desk. The guns weren't there, they were in the wardrobe, where he always kept them. There was a small case of tools – jewellers' tools.

He heard the man talking.

He went to the window and shouted: 'Police!' and then turned to the door, tools in hand. He had lost precious seconds – but if the man were going to shoot right away, he would have fired a second shot by now.

Mannering began to work on the lock.

He knew its mechanics, but that in itself was frightening.

He had to keep his hands steady.

The lock wasn't quite burglar-proof, he'd seen its weakness when he had examined it, had always judged that it would take five or six minutes to open if one found exactly the right spot.

He kept on working.

He was cold from head to foot.

The police would be here soon, but the front door was locked, it would take them some time to break that down. And once they started the man in the other room would probably shoot.

He was still talking.

Mannering worked with desperate calmness.

Courtney went into the sitting room, swaggering, gun thrust forward. Lorna confronted him, but with his free hand, he swept her aside.

Courtney's face was unshaven, his hair dishevelled and plastered about his forehead.

Behind Anne, he saw a table on which were bottles and glasses. He said to Lorna: 'You there—go and pour me out a whisky-and-soda.'

He could cover her at the same time as Anne. As she moved towards the table, he watched Anne more closely. Fear had given a fresh vitality to her beauty.

He said: 'Hallo, sweetheart, I've caught up with you at last. I thought I told you to hide that suit-case and do nothing about it.'

Anne didn't answer.

'Well, you've made your mistake. If you'd done what I told you, you would have lived a long happy life of luxury. Now—'

Lorna had the whisky bottle in her hand.

She raised it, to throw.

Courtney moved the gun round, and fired. The bottle splintered; the shot and the explosion of breaking glass rang out deafeningly. The room was filled with the pungent smell of spirit.

Courtney said: 'Anne, my pretty, let me tell you something. I killed Allen. Today I killed a stranger on a bicycle, because he was after me, and after that I killed Bryce. Maybe I killed others. Now I'm going to kill you.'

He fired.

The bullet went wide: he meant it to. Anne screamed and backed away. Lorna grabbed another bottle, and Courtney fired at her. The bullet went through the cuff of her sleeve.

Courtney sneered at her.

'You want to go to heaven too? That suits me. There isn't a thing you or anyone else can do, I'm just in the mood for making it a hat trick. Three in a row—the maid—you—and my dearest Anne.'

Chapter Twenty-Seven

Head Wound

Mannering heard the second shot; he heard the man talking. He could feel cold sweat on his forehead, neck and lips. The hand holding the tool was moist.

He couldn't hurry; if he hurried, he would spoil his chance of forcing the lock.

He heard another shot, followed by a cry and, almost immediately, by a fourth shot.

Sweat rolled down his forehead and a drop splashed on to the back of his hand. The tool was holding firm and he began to turn it in the lock. The lock moved. If the tool slipped, he would be back where he started.

The lock clicked back.

He drew away, and turned the handle; and heard only the man's voice. He didn't know what had happened, who had been hurt. He opened the door, and Courtney's voice sounded clearer.

'In a row—the maid—you—and my dearest Anne.'

Courtney stood with his back to the open door of the sitting-room. Lorna was out of sight, Mannering could just see Anne's head and the top of her face.

He could see Courtney's gun.

'I've plenty of ammunition, and another gun,' Courtney said.

There was a thud downstairs, then a series of thuds. Courtney heard the noise, and said softly: 'Your friends are arriving, Anne, but they won't get me. When I've finished you, I'll kill myself.'

He levelled the gun.

Mannering leapt.

He had two yards to cover from a standing start. He saw Anne's face, transfixed with fear, and caught a glimpse of Lorna's. Then Courtney sensed or heard him, and swung round. Mannering smashed a fist towards his face, and heard the roar of a shot at the same time. He felt Courtney yield beneath his blow, but otherwise felt nothing. He saw the man sprawl backwards and flung himself on him. Courtney still held the gun and struggled madly, bringing his knee up into Mannering's groin. There was a loud thudding at the hall door.

'Open it, Anne!' cried Lorna. 'Open it!'

Mannering gasped: 'Lorna! Get away.'

Courtney's face was a few inches away from his, lips turned back and teeth showing. The veins and muscles in his neck seemed knotted, and he writhed and twisted – and still held the gun. Mannering tried to force his hand away, but Courtney turned the gun towards him, finger on the trigger. Lorna shouted. He prayed that she would go away.

A short roared out, its flash almost blinding. He felt the heat of it – but no pain. He saw blood on Courtney's head, near the temple, and felt him go limp. He sprawled forward, on top of the man. For a moment he felt sick, and weak at the knees. It wasn't until Lorna began to cry his name that he forced himself to struggle up.

He was aware of men running in, and realized that Anne had opened the front door. He dashed a hand in front of his eyes, and saw Courtney clearly, lying with blood oozing from a wound in his head, his eyes closed, his lips slack, and the gun close to his outflung hand.

'Not bad,' said Chittering, an hour later. 'Not bad at all, John. You're learning.'

He tried to be flippant and it was a miserable failure: he might be flippant with Anne, but never about her. She was with Lorna in the spare room, where Ethel was being attended by a doctor. A bullet had gone through her shoulder but she was in no danger.

Courtney was dead.

A message had been telephoned to Bristow, but he hadn't yet turned up. The Yard men who had been on duty outside were over-anxious to be helpful. So were two who had arrived as reinforcements at the same time as a squad car had reached Green Street. Within ten minutes of that call the house had been surrounded – and, as the sergeant in charge said gloomily, that was several minutes too late.

Mannering, not hurt at all, felt pleasantly tired.

Lorna said: 'I think it was the worse few minutes I've ever had. He looked—' she broke off, and glanced towards the door. 'He *was* mad.'

'We'll say mad, out of charity,' Chittering said, 'but if you ask me, he was mostly bad. I've discovered one or two things about him, John. My editor told me to dig as deep as I could, and did I dig!'

'What did you unearth?' inquired Mannering.

Chittering shrugged. 'Everything in the way of muck, blackmail and extortion. There's one little thing that will interest you. Remember you were attacked when you were in Courtney's flat the first time you really stuck your neck out?'

'I do!'

'It was George Renway,' said Chittering, 'a chap he'd been blackmailing. Courtney had been putting the pressure on Winifred Cartwright, a young married woman who'd once made a fool of herself. Renway decided to go and try to get the evidence, in the form of letters. I told him he needn't worry about them any more. You'll put him and the girl out of their misery, won't you?'

'The first chance I get, yes,' promised Mannering. 'Well, that seems to tie up most of the ends, until Bristow comes.'

'And when he does, it'll probably mean an all-night sitting,' said Chittering. 'Er—seeing how things are, and knowing you're overcrowded, suppose I take Anne out to dinner, as promised. I only need twenty minutes to turn in my story, and less than five to ask her if she'll marry me—'

'Blessings on you both,' said Lorna gently.

Twenty minutes later, a brisk and youthful-looking Bristow, was shaking Mannering's hand with unaccustomed vigour.

'You can rate this as the best job you've done,' he declared. 'And the cleanest.'

'Perhaps,' murmured Mannering nostalgically, 'but I've enjoyed others a lot more.' He glanced at Lorna; he had seldom seen her look so free from strain. 'Mean of me to say that Bill,' he added impulsively. 'What'll you drink?'

'What do we drink to?' asked Lorna.

Bristow said: 'To the new leaf, and may it never wither.'

Rather solemnly, the three raised their glasses to their lips.

Bristow was the last to put his down. 'Well, I had a word with Chittering downstairs, I gather he's told you something. The rest of it doesn't need much telling. We've held Morris, and he's made a complete statement. He was in it with Bryce from the beginning. He blames Bryce for all the violence, of course, and says he himself was just the channel through which stolen jewels were bought and sold. Bryce went into this with Larmont soon after he sold you the Fesinas, John—and he'd been planning it for some time. It started some years ago when a client of Bryce's died intestate, and proved to have a few jewels he'd no right to. Bryce sounded Larmont, who bought them. After that Bryce kept up supplies pretty regularly. They used Reginald Allen and Courtney as strong-arm men.'

Mannering said: 'Where does Lady Larmont come in?'

'As far as I can gather, she told you the truth. She started to blackmail them but was very amateur in some ways. The men planned to raid Quinns. Then she came along, said she could get duplicate keys of Larmont's strong-room, and suggested a raid there, telling Bryce where the electric control could be switched off. It meant throwing Larmont over, but according to Morris, Bryce was ready to do that. He got her to give him the keys, and passed them on to Courtney. All would have gone well for them if you hadn't been at the house.'

Lorna said slowly: 'What about Larmont?'

'I don't think there's much hope, either for us or for him,' said Bristow. 'We've had a good brain man to have a look at him. He was always on the borderline of sanity, victims of jewel-mania usually are!' Bristow gave Mannering a sly look, which finished up as a broad grin.

'So we can call it a day,' Mannering said, with deep relief.

Bristow said a little awkwardly: 'I'm just a policeman, and I know my limitations. They aren't all because of rules and regulations, but a lot of them are. Given a man who will take a few chances but keep me advised all along the line, I think we could get many results more quickly than we do now, and perhaps get some we wouldn't otherwise get at all. That's almost heresy for a policeman, but you heard me!' He stood up. 'You're going to keep the new method up, aren't you?'

Mannering was smiling, a long, but happy smile,

'I'll try,' he said.

JOHN CREASEY

GIDEON'S DAY

Gideon's day is a busy one. He balances family commitments with solving a series of seemingly unrelated crimes from which a plot nonetheless evolves and a mystery is solved.

One of the most senior officers within Scotland Yard, George Gideon's crime solving abilities are in the finest traditions of London's world famous police headquarters. His analytical brain and sense of fairness is respected by colleagues and villains alike.

'The finest of all Scotland Yard series' – New York Times.

GIDEON'S FIRE

Commander George Gideon of Scotland Yard has to deal successively with news of a mass murderer, a depraved maniac, and the deaths of a family in an arson attack on an old building south of the river. This leaves little time for the crisis developing at home ....

'Gideon of Scotland Yard emerges as one of the most real working detectives in modern fiction.... A sympathetic and believable professional policeman.' - New York Times

JOHN CREASEY

THE CREEPERS

"The prisoner's hand was thin and bony ... And in the centre of the palm was a pinkish mark. It was the shape of a wolf's head, mouth open, fangs showing. Although it was what he had expected to see, Inspector West felt a twinge of repugnance a stab not unrelated to fear. It was the fifth time he had seen the mark of the wolf – the mark of Lobo."

A gang of cat burglars led by Lobo cause mayhem as they terrorize the city. They must be stopped, but with little in the way of evidence the police are baffled. Just how can Inspector West manage to do this in what is a race against time before more victims succumb?

"Here is an excellent novel of law enforcement officers, harried, discouraged and desperately fatigued, moving inexorably ahead under the pressure of knowledge that they must succeed to save human lives." - Cleveland Plain-Dealer

"Furiously exciting" - Chicago Tribune

"The action is fast, continuous and exciting" - San Francisco News

JOHN CREASEY

THE HOUSE OF THE BEARS

Standing alone in the bleak Yorkshire Moors is Sir Rufus Marne's 'House of the Bears'. Dr. Palfrey is asked to journey there to examine an invalid - who has now disappeared. Moreover, Marne's daughter lies terribly injured after a fall from the minstrel's gallery which Dr. Palfrey discovers was no accident. He sets out to investigate and the results surprise even him . . . .

"'Palfrey' and his boys deserve to take their places among the immortals." - Western Mail

INTRODUCING THE TOFF

Whilst returning home from a cricket match at his father's country home, the Honourable Richard Rollison - alias The Toff - comes across an accident which proves to be a mystery. As he delves deeper into the matter with his usual perseverance and thoroughness , murder and suspense form the backdrop to a fast moving and exciting adventure.

'The Toff has been promoted to a place of honour among amateur detectives.' – The Times Literary Supplement

Printed in Great Britain
by Amazon